"Can be compared with J. D. Salinger's

'CATCHER IN THE RYE'

remarkable . . . qualities of imagination,
suspense, terror . . ."

—Harrison Smith, *Saturday Review*

"A haunting journey, in the lengthening shadow of fear, has both its heartache and its horror . . . there's warmth here as well as cold dread."

—Virginia Kirkus' *Bulletin*

"Rises to a climax as violent and breathtaking as Stevenson could have devised . . ."

—San Francisco *Chronicle*

THE FOOL KILLER was originally published by Doubleday & Company, Inc.

PRAISE FOR THE AUTHOR...
AND HER BOOK

THE
FOOL
KILLER

By HELEN EUSTIS

Popular Library • New York

POPULAR LIBRARY EDITION
Published in February, 1964

Copyright, 1954, by Helen Eustis
Library of Congress Catalog Card Number: 54-5167

Published by arrangement with Doubleday & Company, Inc.
Doubleday & Company edition published in February, 1954
First printing: December, 1953

DEDICATION

To the memory of my father,

HAROLD CLAYPOOLE EUSTIS

and to my son,

ADAM EUSTIS FISHER

THEM
1

When I come home I knowed the Old Crab was waiting for me, and I would catch it. I kicked around the yard a time, but it was cold out there; the dark was falling, the light looked warm and yellow in the kitchen windows, so I give up and went inside. She was by the stove stirring something; I tried to sneak past, but she reached out and catched me by the ear.

"Where you think *you're* going, pray?" she says, and I knowed I was in for it. When she'd call me "sir," mostly it was a clout on the ear, but when she'd say "pray," it was a licking, sure and certain.

"It's ruint," she says. "You know that, don't you?"

I looked at the buttons on her waist, holding my head **still** so's my ear wouldn't pull, and I says, "Yes'm."

"It's ruint so's you couldn't even use the parts," she says, "and furthermore, there's a spoke knocked out of the wagon wheel."

I didn't say nothing. I stopped looking at her buttons and started to looking at my shoes, which was a old pair of hers, all stretched and shaped like her feet. I'd never of had them on, only there was a late frost the night before, and she'd catched me before I got out the house barefoot in the morning.

"Who's going to pay for it, tell me that?" she says. "Who you reckon will pay for a new one, pray?"

I didn't do nothing but squinch up my toes inside the shoes. "What was the last thing I said to you after milking last night?" she says.

"Put it away," I says, only when my voice come out it didn't make no sound.

"Speak up," she says, giving my ear a pull, "and look me in the eye when you answer me!"

I looked in her face. Her mouth was like the edge of the butcher knife, straight and sharp; she had the red spots on her neck that always come there when she was mad, and her eyes was so mean I thought I seen sparks in them. "You said to put it away," I says, out loud this time.

"Put it away I said, and put it away I meant, but there you left it for your pa to run over with the wagon this morning, and that's fifteen dollars throwed away if it's a cent."

I dropped my head in spite of her twisting my ear, and I says, "He ain't my pa," but it come out louder than I meant.

"What's that?" she hollers, giving my ear a terrible jerk.

Then I felt kind of wild, and I yelled right up in her face, "He ain't my pa, and you ain't my ma!"

She let go my ear then, and slapped my face, first on one cheek with the palm of her hand, then on t'other, with the back. "I'm going to whale the tar out of you!" she says, leaning over and spitting the words right in my face.

They was tears in my eyes from the slaps, and I knowed I'd bawl before she was through, because some way I never could keep from it, but I stared right back at her and says, "That ain't news!" like I felt bold as brass. She could lick me, all right, but there wasn't no need for her to know I was licked.

She was a tall skinny woman with bones sticking out all over, and nothing round to her where you could notice it, but, like the Old Man used to say, she was tough as a catamount and could lick like fury when she got her temper up. Once I put newspapers in my pants, but they made a whacking noise so she caught on. She kept a stock of switches behind the kitchen dresser just for me. Now she went and grabbed one, whipping it through the air so it thrupped, and, grabbing me by the ear once more, she dragged me through the cold hall and into the parlor. It was chilly there, too, and dark and funny-smelling from being shut up.

"Take down your pants," she says, and stamps out of the room.

6

I started to take them down, but my hands was shaking so I didn't have the buttons undone before she come back with the kitchen lamp. I wasn't scared. I just couldn't stop the shaking.

"Take 'em down, I said," she yells at me, "and lay over that stool!"

I done what she told me, and she begun to whack. They wasn't nothing I could do. She had me bellering like a lost calf before she was through. I ain't no crybaby. When I fell out the loft and busted my arm, I never cried a drop, though I may of winced some. It's only lickings when I can't keep it down. It used to shame me terrible in them days, but later on, when I told Milo about it once, he explained to me how it could be like some folks busts out with a rash from strawberries, or has the nightmare if they eat cheese. Wasn't like I was a coward. Milo said he'd seen growed men go through battle whooping like wild Injuns, and faint like a girl if you taken a sliver out of their finger. Hadn't nothing to do with being scared.

"That ought to learn you!" she'd say ever little while, but mostly she'd save her breath. By the time she stopped, she was panting and I was blubbering.

"Pull up your pants," she says. "Go to your room. No supper for you."

I climbed the stairs, hiccuping some and holding up my pants. It was cold in my room, and dark, and I hadn't a light for the candle, but outside the window you could see stars. I laid across the bed and howled for a time more, knowing she couldn't hear me down in the kitchen, and the Old Man wasn't yet back from town. The worst of it all was I knowed it was a fool thing I done myself, and I was ashamed. I meant to put it away, I swear. If she'd of give me a chance, I'd told her I was sorry—only what good would that have been? Fifteen dollars, and already they'd spent a plenty raising me, and me nothing but a thorn in their side. I hated them, but I wasn't so unreasonable I couldn't see that.

Then all of a sudden it come over me that this time I'd go. You ever been took by a idea that way? Oh, many's the time I'd thought of it before—how I'd sneak over the woodshed roof some dark night and be off and away. I'd start out for Passerel and be there in time for the 12:47 train. Then I'd ride the cars to some far-off place and start all over again. Maybe I'd go West, searching for gold; I'd come back a rich man, able to pay off all I owed them and not be beholden any more . . . Only this time it come to me like a sort of shiver in my innards that I really meant it for sure.

What's the use fooling around? I thought. *I ain't no use to them, and I got no use for them. They took me in when I was a orphan; they gave me victuals and clothes, thinking I'd grow up useful—but I ain't, and I hate the both of them, so what's the use to stay? It'd only be him praying over me and her licking me to Judgment Day.*

I fell asleep thinking it, as I had many a night before; what was different, I woke up thinking it, too, and it wasn't morning, but late in the night; I waked up because I had fell asleep outside the covers with my clothes on, and was cramped and cold. The stars shone bright, the house was still, and I thought: *I'm going now! I'm running away!* Just then I heard the parlor clock strike twelve with its old twangy chime. I got up and pulled the wedge out of the window sash. It was stuck some from being closed all winter, but I got it up. The peepers in the marsh across the road was jingling like a million sleigh bells. I climbed out on the woodshed roof as easy as I could and dropped to the ground. I sat down on the earth when I was down and unlaced her old shoes. I took them round to the back door and set them on the sill. They looked like two mean old women, sitting there in the starlight with their uppers flopped over; I stuck my tongue out at them. The barn cat come out of the shadows and meowed at me; I told her, "Goodbye, Tab," in a whisper.

Then I snuck round under the lilac bushes and out the front gate into the road. My feet was still tender from the winter so's the stones hurt some, but it wasn't too cold. I stepped right along and got to Passerel in plenty of time for that train.

DIRTY JIM JELLIMAN
2

I never had no trouble at all getting on that train. I got to it just in time; it was pulled up as if 'twas waiting for me, with the bell dinging and the engine giving off quiet chuffs like a giant breathing, the brakeman swinging his lantern, and the engineer

8

leaning out the cab to spit onto the platform. First thing I seen was a boxcar with the door open; I slipped inside and it was empty as a drum. It was so easy it looked like God meant for me to go.

That was a queer night all right. When I'd wake, I'd think I was dreaming, and when I'd sleep, I'd dream so real I'd think I was awake. I dreamed the Old Man come home and licked me, too; I dreamed something about a church; I dreamed Tab had kittens and I run over them with the wagon. At last I woke up and seen it was day; the train was stopped, but when I looked out, it didn't seem to be stopped no place particular; I reckoned there must be a water tank on the other side the cars somewheres. What I had on my mind the most was that I had to go somewheres something powerful; I looked up and down to see was they any trainmen in sight, and when I seen they wasn't, I slid out the crack of the door and jumped. They was a gravel bank which I rolled down; below it was a mess of bushes, which I took advantage of.

The birds was singing all around; the engine was just steaming easy, sending white clouds up in the blue sky, and I commenced to feel fine. *I done it*, I thought. *That's one thing they'll have to say, whatever happens. I done it* . . . I set out to climb back up that steep gravelly bank, slipping and sliding and scrambling. Then all at once the engine give a big snort, and the train begun to move.

"Hi!" I yelled, before I even thought, just like I had a right to ask that train to wait for me. I dug in toes and fingers, knees and elbows, whatever was handy or could grip, but by the time I got to the top, the end of the caboose was staring me in the face from quite a ways away, and getting littler all the time. I could see the brakeman standing out on the back step, and when he seen me, too, he looked so surprised it was comical. Then he pulled out his red handkerchief and give me a wave. I guess he never knew I rode all night on his train.

I was left standing on the track, feeling like there was nothing in that place to meet God's eye but me and that water tower. The tracks was on a embankment; on the one side I could see a river twisting through a tufty stretch of marshland; on the other, behind the water tower, was a ridge with a stand of saplings on it, like the hair on a hog's backbone. They was nothing but the tracks and the tower to show there was any man alive in the world besides me. *Well*, thinks I, *if I follow the tracks, they're bound to cross a road . . . I reckon . . . Somewheres in the next hundred miles* . . . So I put my hands in my

9

pockets and started out to walk the ties. But my stomach felt awful empty to last a hundred miles. Was *they* up yet? I wondered. Land yes, the sun was seven o'clock high. He'd of come in from the chores, and she'd be stirring the porridge, with the coffee setting back on the stove. *Where's that limb of Satan?* he'd say, and she'd answer, *You mean he warn't out there with you?* Or, no. That wouldn't be how it was. When he went out the kitchen door, he'd of been bound to stumble on the shoes.

I was lucky that day. I didn't more than round the bend where the tracks curved about the ridge than I seen a crossing sign, standing up white and pretty down the line. *Watch out for the cars!* I knowed it said. "Watch out for George Mellish!" I says out loud, and I felt like a big old engine with my pistons working and my steam a-spouting. I whistled for the crossing, and a whole flock of crows rose out of a oak tree. One of them come down on the track a ways ahead and cocked his head at me, settling his wings, bold as brass. Crows is such a knowing bird. I felt like this one had found out all about me, how I'd run away and all, and was looking me over careful with his beady eye, getting ready to report back to headquarters, like a Johnny Reb spy. Maybe he'd fly back to the Old Crab and tell her where I was, and her and the Old Man'd git in the wagon and come after me. I run at him and waved my arms. "Shoo!" I yells. "Scat! Git on out of here!" He looked at me kind of impudent, taking his time, but finally he opened out his wings and flapped away.

When I come to the crossing, then it was a puzzle to know which direction to turn. To the left was just flat and barren marshland as far as the eye could see; to the right was a kind of hillock, and the road took a turn; I went that way, thinking mabe there would be a house behind the rise where they'd let me chop wood, or water the stock, or something for my breakfast. As I walked, I begun thinking of pieces of bread with thick butter, or coffee with lots of sugar and cream, or a mess of eggs with some frizzled ham. But they wasn't a house nowhere in sight. Not round that bend, nor the next one, nor the next one . . . *It's a road,* I kept telling myself. *It's got to go somewheres.*

And then, didn't I round yet another bend and find that that road never went nowheres at all? Leastways, all it went to was the dooryard of a house, and there it stopped and went no further.

Which would have been all right, too, only the house was plumb plain deserted, as anybody could see.

10

Once it had been yellow, but the paint was all wore down to the wood, so now it was mostly browny, with a little yellow left on, not in patches, but more like a all-over shine. Half the window panes was broke, and the shutters hung ever which ways so it looked like if you sneezed, half of them would of fell off. The porch was broke in, too. Hadn't nobody lived there in years. I knowed I'd have to turn round and take the road back to the tracks and across that dreary marshland. I don't mind saying I felt bad . . . *If I'd snuck up on that crow kind of easy,* I thought, *maybe I could of catched him and wrung his neck. Then I coulda built a fire . . . I might trap a rabbit, but it would take a powerful long time, most likely . . . She could of give me supper, anyways, seeing she licked me . . . She could of made it one or t'other.*

I was so empty that just *thinking* about that licking could of made me bawl, and discouraged, too, and my feet was beginning to get sore. *Well,* thinks I, *maybe there'll be a pump out back of the house, and I can get a drink there, anyways.*

So I kept on down the road to the house. Once I thought I seen something slip through the tall dead grass in the yard like it was a cat, and I wondered if maybe the folks hadn't been gone from there as long as it looked like, but then I decided most likely it was a skunk or a possum or so that I seen . . . Quiet it was, the way only a empty house can be quiet, and I was glad I had come there in broad day . . . I went around to the back of the house, and, sure enough, there was a rusty old pump, with a white china cup laying on the ground by it. Behind the house a ways I seen a sorry-looking old barn, with a oak woods behind, and off to one side a privy with the door swinging open.

And setting inside that privy, just as big as life, was a old man reading a book!

I thought I should jump out of my skin!

And while I was standing there, as you might say froze, he looks up and says, "Howdy!" calm as you please!

He was a old, old codger, with a long beard which would of been white if he hadn't been the dirtiest old man I ever seen. Everything about him was so dirty it was almost green, excepting his blue, blue eyes. He had a old hat on his head with a hole tore in the brim, and he wasn't doing nothing private in that privy at all.

"Come on in and set down," he says to me. "I always set here of a pleasant morning—in the sun and out of the wind. Where you appear from, boy? You ain't one of the Treadway younguns, that I know. They all got that undershot lower lip like the old man."

I was plain dumfounded to find a living human being there. I come closer to him, looking pretty foolish, I reckon, with my mouth hanging open. The onliest thing that come to my mind to say was, "You got your book upside down."

"That's on account of I got upside-down eyes," says the old codger.

I felt more turned round than ever, and I says, "What you mean, you got upside-down eyes?"

"I know you wouldn't hardly notice it," he says, "but the Lord had a little accident and set 'em in upside down. Take you, for instance. Might's well be walking on the ceiling, far as I'm concerned."

Then I knowed he was either joshing me, or touched in the head; I hoped it was the first and not the last.

He shut up his book and come out of the privy then. He smelled kind of powerful when he come near.

"What's your name, boy?" he says. "Where you from? Bet you're running away."

How do you reckon he'd know? I was feeling so foolish and lightheaded I thought maybe that crow'd flown on ahead and told him all about me.

"My name's George Mellish," I says, "and I'd be much obliged if I could have a drink from your pump."

"Help yourself," he says. "Nice-mannered boy, too. Where's your folks boy?"

"Dead," I says, which was true.

"Well, now, George, ain't that a shame! The Lord giveth, and the Lord taketh away. Bet you're hungry."

"Yes, *sir!*" says I, trying to keep from sounding too greedy.

"Well, come along then, George. Ain't got much, but what I got I'm glad to share. Sure is a treat to have company, long as it ain't women."

So I set down the cup and followed him inside.

3

I'm here to tell you that house was a pure mess. I never seen nothing like it. I would have give my shirt to have the Old Crab stick her nose in it, since I was the filthiest boy she ever saw . . . So she kept saying . . .

They was a cat smell and a human smell and a victuals smell, and they wasn't none of them sweet. They was heaps of things in corners and under the sink, like corncobs and apple cores and peach pits, and then things all moldered over so that you wondered what they was, and then thought you'd be just as well off not to know. They was cobwebs in the corners that widders could of made mourning veils out of. They was pieces of broke china and wads of chewed-up tobacco—well, I can't tell you the least of it!

"Ain't it gorgeous?" the old man says.

What was I to say? Don't get no false ideas that I'm a clean boy. I wouldn't say it, because it wouldn't be so. But that place beat me.

He began rustling around in cupboards, meantime chattering along, not waiting for a answer.

"Now *you* don't know why I call it gorgeous," he says. "That's because *you* never seen it before. So I'll tell you how it was. Clean as a whistle it was—*then*. Smelled like soap and looked like glass. In them days it was, 'My land, don't knock your pipe out there!' or 'Take them dirty boots off before you come in my kitchen,' and tobacco! Had to go up in the woods to take a chaw!

"Well, sir, she died. Quick and easy, it was; musta been a relief to her, too. Kinda mean woman, anyhow, had no children to soften her up, and I guess I taken the starch out of her . . . Yessir, she died. Well, sir, George, I come back from the funeral; I looked at this here house, and it was neat as a pin. I stood smack dab in the middle of the parlor, and I says my own name out loud. 'Jim,' I says. 'Jim.' Like that. And I ain't done a thing I didn't want to since. Let the land grow wild and hire out

13

to neighbors when I'm low on cash. Ain't had a bath since the night I was drunk and fell in the creek . . .

"So that's why I say it's gorgeous. Yessir, when I come in this here house and see how disgusting it all is, I just heave a sigh and say, 'Ain't it gorgeous!' Yessir, that's what I say ever time, to kinda let the good Lord know I'm grateful for His mercies and His blessings.

"Well, you wouldn't understand, I reckon. You being such a young feller, maybe you never suffered like me from a clean woman."

"Well," I says, cautious like, "in a manner of speaking I have. You might say."

The old man had out a loaf of bread and a jug of molasses. He taken the coffeepot and filled it from a can of water. It kind of shivered me to see his hands on that bread. He sure was one dirty old man. But he kept chattering along all the while he was cutting the bread and making the coffee, like he hadn't had company in a coon's age. Old folks is like that. It's often so.

"Is that true, George?" he says now. "Is that true for a fact? Now ain't that a coincidence, you and me suffering from a clean woman the same. Tell me, George, was that your ma? I reckon you haven't been married yet at your age."

"Oh no, sir," says I, "I ain't but twelve! It weren't my ma. It was folks took me in after my own folks died."

"Is that a fact?" says he. "She was so clean you run away! That's the facts of it, ain't it, George?"

"Well, yes, sir, and no, sir," says I.

"Oh, don't call me sir, call me Dirty," says he. "Dirty Jim Jelliman's my full name, but lately don't nobody call me nothing but Dirty. Now set down," he says, "coffee'll be done in a minute. Here's some bread, help yourself to 'lasses, and tell me how it all come to be."

I tell you, I lit into that food until I'd finished off the heel of the loaf. Wasn't nothing but the molasses to put in the coffee, but I'd of drunk a mud puddle by then. And while I filled my belly, I told him how I was left a orphan, and how him and her took me in and raised me, but how everything come out backwards, somehow. About me, that is to say.

I'd studied on the whole matter a good deal, and I told him first off, like I'da told anyone the same, that I wanted him to understand I wasn't a good boy. Never was and never will be, and that's a fact. Some folks has thought I was bad, and some not so downright terrible, but nobody has never accused me of being outright good. But it appeared to me like what him and

14

her was looking for was some kind of a angel like you read about in those Sunday school stories where the good feller always dies young and gets carried off to heaven. I could never see the profit in that. What use would I of been to them if I'd been so good I'd died young like them good boys you read of?

The Old Man wasn't so awful, except for praying all the time. He had the habit of asking for guidance whenever the spirit moved him—I've seed him drop on his knees in a manure pile without noticing a thing. I disremember what he was praying for that time, but most likely it was for the Lord to give him strength after I'd done some fool thing.

When I was a little feller, I used to *try* to be good. I'd take long spells when I'd say my prayers at night, and when I'd wake up next morning I'd make my mind up, *Now today I'll be good as gold!* Well, them was the times I'd act like a fool. Kick over the milk bucket, drop the eggs, never meaning no harm at all. One day she sent me to town for nothing but a spool of thread. Do you know that when I got there I'd clean forgot what she sent me for? Can you imagine a feller walking three miles for nothing but one little bitty spool of Number 60 white cotton thread with not another thing on his mind, and disremembering what he come for when he got to the store? I almost run away *that* time. Appeared like I wasn't the worth the powder to blow me up with if I was that big of a fool . . . She licked me. Naturally. It come as a kind of a relief to me.

So I give up trying to be good, because it seemed like I felt better when I was outright bad. If she licked me or he prayed over me for sassing back or sneaking off fishing instead of doing the chores, and I knowed I'd done whatever it was apurpose, looked like I didn't feel so bad. Looked like what *I* couldn't stand was when I knowed myself I'd been a fool.

And then I told the fool thing I done that last time and how I come to run away . . . Pshaw, it wasn't the licking! I just couldn't stand it no more, being such a fool!

Dirty Jim listened to me all the while with his head a-bobbing so that ever now and then the end of his beard would dip in his coffee cup, and I'd get kind of throwed off my tale from watching it come out dripping like a paintbrush and him never pay it no mind. Ever now and then he'd say, "Sho!" or, "Is that a fact?" like he never heard nothing like what I was saying before. He sure could listen good when he felt like it. It was like I had a load off my mind when I got through.

"Well, sir, George," he says then, "you surely have had a interesting life, and that's a fact, and you sure have studied on it a

15

heap moren most fellers your age is likely to do. Yessir, I shouldn't be surprised was you to grow up a rich feller and own a bank or like that—if the Fool Killer don't get you first."

"The Fool Killer!" says I. "Who's that?"

"What!" says Dirty Jim, drawing back from the table like he was astonished. "You never heard tell of the Fool Killer?"

"No, sir," says I, "I never have." And just then a cloud come over the sun, turning that dirty old kitchen all dark and gloomy, while at the same time a shiver run down my spine from a goose walking on my grave.

"Oh Lord, George!" says he. "To think a boy could grow to your age so bright and never hear tell of the Fool Killer!"

I looked at Dirty Jim Jelliman, with his green-dirty face with the yellerish whiskers growing out of the grime like seedlings from a cold frame, and his bright blue upside-down eyes . . . What in tunket did he mean, upside-down eyes? . . . And I felt all strange and shivery to think I'd never seen him nor ever been in this place in my life, nor heard of such a thing as a Fool Killer before . . . "Well, who is he?" I says at last. "I'd admire to hear." But the truth is, I wasn't so sure I'd care to know at all.

"Why," says Dirty Jim, "the Fool Killer is a great tall feller —I reckon he must be eight foot or over—tallern any man— and he carries a chopper so sharp it'd cut through a fence post like it was a segar, for chopping fools."

"Chopping fools!" says I. "What's he want to go and do that for?"

"Because that's his line of work," says Dirty Jim. "That's what the Lord made him and set him on earth for. The Lord made cats for killing mice, mice for gnawing stores, stores for feeding folks, and the Fool Killer for killing fools."

"What's fools for?" I wanted to ask, but I didn't, some way. I wished he hadn't of brought the Lord in. Folks don't call the Lord's name when it's just a tale.

"Of course, there wouldn't be no need for the Fool Killer if it wasn't for fools," he goes on. "But there's such a plenty that he never lacks for work. Nosir! Not he! Because whenever the fools gets thick, he's got to clear them out, just like they was weeds. And when the fools gets too *all-fired* thick, why the Fool Killer stirs up a war. Yessir, you may hear how the boys in blue saved the Union and freed the slaves, and, mind you, don't never say Dirty Jim Jelliman said it was a lie! But at the same time, that war there sure did clear out a mess of fools!"

"Well," I says, feeling pretty bad, but resigned, "I certainly

16

never heared of the Fool Killer before, and I ain't met him yet —touch wood!" and I did, "but I reckon he'll get me in the end."

"Oh Great Day, George!" says Jim, leaning forward so's the end of his beard went in the coffee again. "Don't give up so easy, boy! Why, they's plenty of us he misses out on! Look at me! Eighty or ninety if I'm a day!"

That cheered me some to hear Jim call hisself a fool, too, but it didn't what you could call comfort me. If they *was* a Fool Killer—mind you, I ain't a boy to swaller any old tale without chewing on it some—but just supposing there was, wasn't it kind of foolish for the two of us to gather together in the one spot? Just asking for trouble, you might say.

I got up from the table. "I thank you kindly for the victuals," I says. "You sure treated me right. Is there some chores I could do for you, like split some kindling or fetch some water before I be on my way?"

"On your way!" cried Dirty Jim, jumping up, too, so quick he overset his chair. For a old feller, he surely was spry. "My land, George, you ain't going off and leave me when you no moren got here! Course, I know you got to be on your way sooner or later, having your fortune to make and all. But stay a few days and keep a old man company! Seems like I'm already spoiled for lonesomeness, having you to talk to this short while!"

And I felt kind of queer to see his upside-down eyes all shiny with tears. I didn't want to look at him for fear they'd overflow and run down into his beard.

I was of two minds whether to go or stay. Seemed as if I ought to keep going if I was running away. On the other hand, I'd set off in kind of a hurry, without stopping to figure just where I was running to. Mightn't be a bad idea to hole up a day or so and kind of plan my way. Maybe a feller who just set off for nowheres like a bullet shot without aiming would look to— well, might be considered by some folks as a kind of a fool.

Just then, the biggest yellow tomcat I ever seen come running in the back door with his tail straight up in the air, and begun purring and rubbing against my legs so hard he like to knocked me down.

"There!" cries Jim. "That's a sign! That cat'd just as soon claw you to ribbons as look at you! Ain't everbody he takes to that way!"

I knowed the cat probably smelled our Tab on my pants, but he did make me feel kind of at home.

17

"Well," I says, "if you're sure I ain't putting you to no trouble, I'd be proud to visit for a few days."

Dirty Jim jumped up in the air when he heard that, cut a caper, and clapped his hands. "Hallelujah!" he shouts. "Great day in the morning! We'll have us a high old time! We'll kick the bottom right out the bucket! Let's have us a drink of whiskey and celebrate, George!"

"Oh no, sir!" I says, backing off, "I couldn't do that! I taken the pledge!"

4

First off, after I kind of settled down and made up my mind to stay a while at Jim's, I surely did enjoy it. It was so different from where I come from that it made me feel all turned around, sometimes. I'd be setting on the back step in the sun, playing mumblety peg with a jackknife which I had found and Jim said I could keep, or whittling on a stick, when I'd jump up all at once like I'd been shot, forgetting where I was, thinking I heard *her* call me, or that I had forgot something I should of done. Even if you hadn't forgot nothing, she was a woman could always remember something you should of forgot.

Later on, at a time which I will tell about when I come to it, Milo says to me that a boy had ought to try to understand what it's like to be a growed person. Mostly, he says, when folks is mean, it ain't that they hate you personal, it's more likely because they're miserable about something in their own inside. You got to remember how most of the time when they yell at you or get after you, it ain't you they're yelling at at all, but something inside theirselves you never even heard tell of, like some other person has been mean to *them,* or something which they hoped for didn't come true, or they done something they're ashamed even to think of, so they get mad at you just to keep their mind off it. That's how Milo explained it.

Well, I always tried hard to listen to what Milo said, and study on it. He teached me many things, and I will never forget

18

him, whatever may of happened. But sometimes I just had to give up and tell him, "You're a growed man and I ain't but a boy. I guess I just can't get my mind round what you say till I get older." And he would allow how that could be so . . . Be dogged if I could ever understand the Old Crab *or* the Old Man or how it'd feel to be them . . . Ma and Pa, she made me call them, but I can't hardly make myself say that no more. My ma and pa is dead . . . Looked to me like they purely enjoyed it when they ordered a body round and then come to find out he done everything they told him wrong. Anyways, she did. When I done something so's she couldn't find no fault with it—which wasn't moren once in a blue moon—she'd pinch up her lips and say, "Hmp!" like something hurt her, and think up some other thing for me to do right off, so's I could do *that* wrong. As for the Old Man, he used to seem truly sorrowful when he'd thump down on his knees and ask the Lord to look down on me in mercy; could be that I was a genuine thorn in his side. But on the other hand, it appeared to me like if I hadn't been there, plaguey as I was, he'd of got a lot of the tongue lashings from *her* which otherwise was give to me . . . And anyhow, they only took me in so's I'd grow up useful. They didn't have a big place, but it looked like whatever he did prospered. Wet years and dry, whatever was a failing crop, he'd have put in something else instead that thrived on that kind of weather. And she had enough preserves in the cellar to feed the U. S. Army. But they figured it was cheaper to take in a orphan and wait for him to grow up than to hire a hand.

So that was how it was with them—always *Do this,* or *Do that,* while with Jim, it was just, *Do as you please, boy.* With Jim, a body couldn't hardly get in any trouble if he tried, because Jim, he never done nothing he didn't want to, and he expected others to do the same. Mornings, he liked to set out in the privy with the door open, holding a book—upside down or rightside up didn't make no difference to him, unless it had pictures. He was just spinning me a yarn about them upside-down eyes. Jim couldn't read, that was all . . . We ate kind of sketchy, here and there, when we took the notion, and I got to admit that Jim's victuals made me admire the Old Crab for something of a cook. He had a side of smoked meat, and before he was ready for a meal, he'd cut off a chunk, throw it in the pot, and go round gathering greens. Sometimes they was something you'd never guessed a human could eat, but they tasted fine; others, he'd get absent-minded, and once I snatched a bunch of poison ivy out just as he was throwing it in to boil.

He'd bake, too, when the spirit moved him; sometimes *that* would turn out pretty fair, but others it put me in mind of where it says in the Good Book about asking for bread and they give you a stone.

Afternoons he'd drop off to sleep somewheres, or else we'd go fishing in the creek that run through the woods behind the barn, and while we fished, he'd talk along. Got so I didn't listen to him much—he'd just ramble on, calling me by the names of other folks and getting so wound up sometimes that he'd have a bite on his line and not even pull it in. Evenings he'd get out the whiskey jug; we'd pull up our chairs to the stove, put our feet in the oven, and he'd tell tales—of Injuns, or folks he'd known, or things that was plumb impossible to of happened anywheres. When he was sleepy, we'd turn in on our pallets we'd made of dirty old quilts on the parlor floor—though I never knowed why, when they was beds and to spare upstairs. Jim snored something terrible, and it looked like I couldn't get used to it; that or the sleeping on the floor made me lay awake at night a good deal, thinking different thoughts about where I was going and where I'd been. I'd get to feeling anxious, laying there in the dark, for fear whatever I did would just turn out to be some foolishness, and I'd imagine that feller eight foot tall with his sharp chopper; when I'd fall asleep, there he'd be, chasing me down my dreams, like I was a rabbit and he was a hound. I begun to feel a little off my feed, too, which like as not was what give me the dreams. I reckoned I had a touch of spring fever—I'd of been dosed with sulphur and molasses long before this time of year if *she'd* been around.

As the days went by, it begun to hit me what a odd thing it was, living with a person who don't do no work. Jim, of course, he was used to hisself. He could putter round the house for hours, picking things up and laying them down, losing things and finding them again, talking to hisself, or me, or the cat, all the while.

"Gol dang it," I'd hear him mutter, "now where'd she put it? Takes a fool woman to put things where a pirate crew wouldn't of thought of for a hiding place. No, Tom, 'tain't down there—*get* out from under my feet, you fool cat! George, *have* you seen thatair plug? I laid it down somewheres and I've looked high and low—oh, Great Day, there 'tis, right before my eyes —been a snake 'twould have bit me!"

In the beginning I'd answer him when he asked me questions like that, but he never listened to me no more than when he said something to Tom and Tom meowed. And then I used to try and help him look for whatever 'twas he'd mislaid, but it looked like that only made him kind of cranky. He'd shoo me out of the way just like he did the cat . . . He could spend a whole afternoon that way, losing things and finding them—his plug of tobacco, or a spoon, or one of his old wore-out books which he couldn't read. I offered to read him from *Pilgrim's Progress* once, but it looked like that made him crankier than anything. Yet by and large he weren't a cranky old man at all. Only kind of set in his ways, which was to leave him be and he'd leave you be, and not liking to be disturbed from them.

When I couldn't find nothing else to do, I'd explore. In a strange place, a boy can always find a sight of things to explore. If growed folks comes to a house they never been in, they got to sit in the parlor and talk polite, but with a boy, nobody minds if he takes a look around. Course, I knowed better than to pry; I asked Jim first was it all right if I kind of scouted round, and he says, "The place is yours, boy!" So I went in the attic and all over till there wasn't nothing more to see. Jim never went upstairs hisself; that part was just the way his missis had left it, except for what the mice and the mildew and the spiders and the dust had done. But out in the barn the loft was mighty nigh as bad as the downstairs of the house, what with old horse collars, and pieces of harness, a ox yoke, broke-up rakes, rusty plowpoints, and goodness knows what all. I found me some treasures, too, like that jackknife which Jim let me keep, and a cavalry sword with a broke blade from some old war, and a spyglass with no glass in. But pretty soon I'd seed everything twice, just about, and didn't feel curious no more.

From the beginning, I'd split kindling and draw water and fill the wood box without being told, because I was bound to do what I could and not feel beholden, even if Jim *was* such a nice old codger. But right shortly I was so far ahead on the kindling there didn't seem no use splitting any more for a spell. The fact was, time begun to hang heavy on my hands, and I guess it was that put the notion in my mind to swamp up the kitchen a mite one morning when I'd got up before Jim. So I found me a old wore-down broom, brought in a pail of water, and went to work. But when Jim come in and seen me at it, I thought he'd hit the ceiling.

"Good Lord, boy, what are you *at?*" he hollers.

Why, I wasn't doing nothing but pour a little water on the floor and sweep it down! And I'd throwed out some bits of broke china and some apple cores and a pile of corncobs was under the sink. And it wasn't like I hadn't left twice as much as I'd cleared away. But Jim set down at the table and put his head in his hands like I'd busted his whiskey jug.

"George," he says, "you been ruint! I hate to say it, but you been spoiled for manhood. To think the day would come I'd see a red-blooded boy a sweeping of the floor without no woman to drive him to it! If somebody'd told me, I'd of denied it. Not George! I'd of said. He'd as soon wash his ears!"

I reckon I turned red at that. Truth was, I *had* washed my ears, not two days since. When I'd knowed it was Saturday night. Course, I didn't do no such foolish thing as bathe, or wash my feet or nothing, but a kind of feeling come over me—habit, I guess you might call it—and I held my head under the pump and run my shirttail round the creases where the dirt collects. Or so *she* used to say. So it looked to me like what Jim said might be true—that I *was* spoiled for manhood—acting like that with her seventy-five or a hundred miles away!

5

That was my last day at Dirty Jim's, though I never guessed it then, and I reckon I was fixing to sicken all the while. I kind of laid around the whole day, feeling low in my mind and steering clear of Jim, because it really looked like I'd got him riled. He tromped around the house muttering to hisself, losing one thing after another and not finding none of them, complaining of how when you thought you had women nailed down in one spot, up they'd pop in another; the Devil wasn't a patch on a woman; they got their claws in you and never let you go—even that fool Tom off tomcatting after some woman—cat, that was to say—coming back half tore to pieces and imagining he's enjoying life. Oh, nobody need tell James P. Jelliman of the pleasures of the flesh! He'd had em and they'd had him; praise the Lord they was over and done with! Women! . . . And when he'd come across me, he'd glare at me till I begun to feel like he must think I was a woman, too, but he looked so fierce at me I dassn't speak up and tell him 'tweren't so.

But when evening come, he acted like he'd got over his mad;

after we'd ate, he got out the jug and we put our feet in the oven like always; he took a long swallow and set out to tell me a tale.

"Now, George," he says, "I wouldn't want you to think I was mad at you. I know I kinda been on my high horse all day, but it ain't because I'm mad. Nosir, I ain't mad, I'm worrited about you, boy, worrited about your past and worrited about your future. You're a likely boy—as likely a boy as ever I see—but the truth is, you *do* do fool things. Cleaning of the floor! Oh, George! Well, least said, soonest mended. Now I told you about the Fool Killer, and the risks a person can run in that direction. But they's a fate worse than that, George, oh, worser by far!"

Now Jim had never preached me no hell-fire and brimstone up to that time, but he sounded so solemn and holy-like that he put me in mind of the Old Man. So, thinking I seen the direction he was working round to, I says, "Hell, you mean?" to kind of help him along.

But Jim says, "Hell!" looking at me like I was a hopeless idjit and he didn't hardly know what to do with me. "Hell, George! Oh my Lord, what a ignorant boy! What's the Devil, George, answer me that?"

"Well, sir," I kind of stammers, "he's a—he's a sort of black feller, like a nigger, I reckon, only with horns and a tail——"

But I could see that wouldn't do. Jim was shaking his head so his beard waved. "No, no, no!" he cries. "That ain't what I mean! Now take it this way: what *ain't* he, George?"

"Well," I says, thinking hard, but only getting more mixed up than ever, "he ain't a *angel*——"

"Oh my great merciful heavens!" says Jim, clapping his hands to his jaws like he had the toothache. "Now, George! Now just be calm! Now just you set there and don't say another word! Now you try listening to this here tale and see if it don't come clear."

I surely didn't have no notion of what he was getting at, but then, I didn't know what he was getting at more times than this, so I just set back and listened while he told his tale.

"Now listen careful, George, and study on what I'm telling you. This here tale is the tale of a Fool, and how he met up with the Fool Killer, but—well, you'll see.

"This here particular Fool was a fool from the time he was a youngun and couldn't help hisself. He was one of the goldarnedest fools you ever did see. Not only did he bust things and knock things down and forget things, but it looked like he loved to *be* fooled. He kept horsehairs in a jar of water because

23

somebody told him they'd turn to snakes. When he heared that if a boy kissed his elbow, he'd turn into a girl and vicy versy, he didn't think he'd much care to *be* a girl, but he like to bust his arm trying, out of pure foolish curiosity. And tales! The worse lies they was, the bigger his eyes'd get, and the more his jaw'd drop. His folks give up on him after they'd tried to straighten him round a while. His brothers was all sensible enough, but he was a born, dyed-in-the-wool fool.

"Naturally, him being such a fool, the Fool Killer heard about him and come to look him over while he was yet pretty young. The first time was after the Fool sewed chicken feathers on his shirt sleeves and 'tempted to fly from the barn roof. That evening, the Fool Killer made hisself invisible and come to the room where the Fool was laying with a busted collarbone, all wore out and bandaged up. The Fool wasn't even as big as you at the time, George, but the Fool Killer walked all round his bed, smacking his lips and feeling his chopper on his thumb, because he didn't know when he'd seen such a promising fool. Then he went away, because though this fool was sure a jim dandy, the Fool Killer didn't want to pick him while he was yet green.

"But though the Fool Killer had made hisself invisible, the Fool had heared him tramping round the bed, and he was so scared he hollered for his ma. She come running up the stairs, sure he'd fallen out the bed and busted the other collarbone, or the Lord knows what all.

"'Ma, Ma!' cries the Fool. 'There's been a body tramping round my bed, but I couldn't see hide nor hair of him. I'm scared, Ma!'

"'Oh for the land's sakes!' says his ma. 'It was the roof creaking like it always does when the day begins to cool!'

"'No, no, Ma, they was footsteps, just as plain! I swear it, Ma!'

"Well, his Ma had dinner on the stove, and she knowed that if the Fool really got to going, he'd keep her there to Judgment Day. So she come and set on his bed and looked him in the eye. ' 'Twas the Fool Killer, then,' she says, 'come to look you over for a fool, and if you don't mend your ways, he'll get you in the end, sure as you're a foot high!'

"And *that* shut the Fool's mouth all right—he just laid there shaking while she went downstairs. *She* never believed what she was saying—only told it to quieten the Fool—but the Fool believed it, and he was right for once—it was true.

"Well, sir, that wasn't the last time he heard those footsteps

—he was such a reglar fool that he durn near got used to them, but it wasn't till he pretty nigh had his growth that he seed the Fool Killer face to face.

"By that time he was a great big gangling feller about seventeen. One day the calf busted loose and run off when the folks was in the wagon with it tied to the tail gate, fixing to take it to town to sell.

" 'Nothing for it but to leave this here fool behind to round up the critter and drive it in after us,' says the Fool's pa. 'I got business to tend to, and we're late starting already.'

"So the wagon went rattling off while the Fool chased after the calf; he catched it presently, put a halter on it, and started out to town.

"He walked down the road at a right smart clip. By and by he seen two fellers walking towards him. Reglar dudes, they was, all dressed up in city clothes. They hailed the Fool, and asked how far 'twas to the next town. He told them, and then one of the fellers says to him, 'Say, Reuben, that's a pretty calf you got there. Where you going with her?'

" 'My name ain't Reuben and she's a bull,' says the Fool. 'I'm taking him to market to sell.'

" 'Why,' says the feller, 'that's a long walk on a hot day. Maybe you'n me can do business right here. I been looking for a likely calf.'

" 'I don't know,' says the Fool, kinda doubtful, 'I got to meet my pa.'

" 'Pshaw,' says the feller. 'Your pappy'll be proud to see you can drive a bargain like a man.'

" 'What'll you give?' says the Fool.

" 'Why,' says the feller, 'have you heard about Jack and his magical beanstalk?'

"Naturally, loving tales, the Fool had.

" 'You recollect how rich he become just out of that handful of beans?'

"The Fool did.

"Well, the long and short of it was, these fellers had with them a magical pea. They couldn't show the Fool all it was able to do without it was planted like Jack's beans, but to prove it was magical, the one feller set down his cardboard grip, the other took three walnut shells out of his pocket, put the shells on the grip, hid the pea under one, and kept making it invisible. That was proof enough for the Fool. He closed the bargain, shook hands, handed over the calf, and went on to town with the pea in his pocket, dreaming of how rich he was to be.

" 'Twas that night, after he was in bed and laying on his stomach because t'other side was kinda tender where his pa'd licked him with the razor strop, that the Fool first seen the Fool Killer with his own eyes. He was sniveling to himself, big as he was, and ever so often he'd say, 'But he never give me a chance to *plant* it!' when he heared them familiar footsteps. Like I said, he was pretty nigh used to them, but this time something made him look up, and, lo and behold! there was the Fool Killer, invisible no more, but right before his eyes! Oh, it was a terrible sight, I can tell you! Eight foot tall with a big bushy beard, hungry-looking red lips, and that chopper—the Fool was so frighted he fainted dead away.

"But when he come to his senses, he was still right in his own bed where he'd left hisself; the Fool Killer hadn't taken him this time neither, and that was when the Fool vowed he'd change his ways. He knew he couldn't help being a natural fool, but to save hisself whatever foolishness he could, he swore he'd only do what his ma and pa told him, and he'd never believe another soul, whatever they was to say. So a few years passed quiet for him, but then his ma went to her reward, and then his pa; first one of his brothers married and bought a place of his own, and then another, till there was only the Fool and his one brother left on the old farm. Then bad luck begun to dog them; that year was a terrible drought; the following was so wet the seeds washed out of the ground; the year after the barn burned; after that, the Fool's brother says to the Fool, 'Let's sell the farm and move to Nebrasky before we starve.'

" 'I won't do it,' says the Fool. 'Last thing Pa said to me before he died was, "Live quiet and stick to the farm." '

" 'Well, if you won't, you won't,' says the brother, after he'd cussed a while. 'We'll have to mortgage the place.'

"So they mortgaged the farm, but bad luck was still after them; first thing they knew, the bank had foreclosed. 'I'm going now,' the brother says. 'If I'd gone when I wanted, it woulda been with full pockets instead of empty, but I'm going, anyhow. Are you coming with me?'

" 'Pa said live quiet and stick to the farm,' says the Fool.

" 'You dang fool,' says his brother, 'they *ain't* no more farm.'

"But the Fool wouldn't budge a inch; he watched his brother pack up his things and go, and that night, alone in the old homestead, he seed the Fool Killer once more.

"This time the Fool Killer walks right in the kitchen door, bending his head to get in. 'Well,' he says to the Fool in a voice that sounded like thunder rolling, 'are you ready to go?'

"The Fool drops down on his knees on the kitchen floor and clasps his hands. 'Oh, don't take me yet, Mr. Fool Killer!' he prays.

"'I'd like to know why not,' says the Fool Killer, 'you being one of the richest, ripest specimens of fool I ever seed!'

"'Oh, don't take me now!' begs the Fool, his eyes shut and his limbs trembling. 'I'll do better, I swear!'

"At that, the Fool Killer begun to rub his chin. 'Hmm,' he says, and walks round the Fool where he was kneeling on the floor, inspecting him on all sides. 'I dunno but you got a point there. You being already such a extraordinary fool, how do I know you won't get better yet? I've a good mind to leave you on the vine for another little while.'

"'Oh, please do, Mr. Fool Killer!' says the Fool. 'Please!'

"And the upshot was that the Fool Killer shouldered his chopper and went away.

"Well, the farm was sold, and the Fool was obliged to move out. He went into town and lived from hand to mouth on odd jobs, till one day a widder woman who lived out to the end of town heared about him and hired him to do her chores in exchange for board and room.

"She was a skinny old witch with a face like a meat ax and a voice like a buzz saw, and from the minute the Fool come in her house, he couldn't do nothing to suit her. From morning to night, it was, 'You great fool, that ain't the way!' or, 'Great heavens look down in mercy and give me patience with this here fool!' The Fool couldn't hardly get out of her sight, and from the day he moved in, it was like a weight had rolled off his shoulders—because with her after him like that all the while, what chance did he have of doing something to bring the Fool Killer round?

"Then one Sunday the widder woman come back from church making a long face, and said folks was looking at her slantwise because she was living alone with a young man in her house, and her not more than in her riper years. The Fool's tongue clove to the roof of his mouth for fear she'd say next that he'd have to go. But she never; just switched and sashayed about kind of extra while she was making dinner, and then finally says, 'Oh my Lord, I never seen such a great fool! Can't you see there's something we got to *do*?' And when the Fool says he didn't know what 'twas, she says, 'Get married, of course.'

"So the next day the Fool put on his Sunday suit, hitched the mare up to the buggy, and drove the widder to the justice of the peace, her nagging him about how the harness was cleaned all the way. They was married proper; she paid for the license, and the Fool drove the both of them home, almost jumping for joy. He seen hisself safe from the Fool Killer for a long time to come—anyways until she died, and she weren't more than twice the Fool's age, and tough to boot.

"But that night when the Fool was all tucked up cozy in the widder's bed, with her teeth on the washstand and her hair on the dresser, what did he hear under the window but them old familiar footsteps.

"'Oh my lord!' he cried. 'Save me, Miz Hawkins, he's after me again!'

"'Shut up and go to sleep, you great fool!' says she. 'Ain't nothing to hear but the wind in the pines.'

"And, sure enough, the Fool did hear a kind of big sighing sound, only it sounded like it was saying words to him, and them words was, 'Poor Fool! Poor Fool!'

"Well, the Fool just laid there a-shaking, thinking that if the Fool Killer had taken to pitying him, his day was surely at hand, and that all his thinking he could escape was just foolishment once more. He laid there listening till he couldn't stand it—that big soughing voice saying, 'Poor Fool! Poor Fool!' over and over, and at last he sneaked out the bed, run down the stairs in his nightshirt and bare feet, and opened the front door. Sure enough, there was the Fool Killer, chopper and all.

"'All right,' says the Fool. 'I mighta knowed it. Take me quick, Mr. Fool Killer, so maybe it won't hurt so bad.'

"But the Fool Killer just shaked his head and says, 'Poor Fool, poor Fool! I ain't come to take you, boy, I come to bid you goodbye!'

"'Bid me goodbye!' says the Fool, not believing his ears.

"The Fool Killer shaked his head some more. 'If I coulda guessed this would happen, I'da taken you before. Now you done passed out of my jurisdiction for good and all. A good, clean, Christian, church-going woman has got you, and next to her anything I could do for you would be child's play!' And with that the Fool Killer disappeared from before the Fool's eyes, never to be seen no more.

"And many was the time in years to come when the Fool come to recognize what he had got hisself in for that he went out on the stoop in the middle of the night and cried, 'Oh, Mr. Fool Killer, come back and get me, please!'

"But the only thing that ever answered him was that kind of

soughing, like the wind in the pines, that seemed to say, 'Poor Fool, poor Fool!' "

Jim stopped there, and reached down for the jug, which was how I knowed it was the end of the tale. Like a lot of tales he told, it didn't exactly seem like it was ended to me. I mean, it was interesting and all, but I couldn't just see what it was all about. Still, it give me a kind of shiver down my spine. The wind was kind of whooping round the corner outside the kitchen, and I could imagine how it might be saying, "Poor Fool, poor Fool!" like in the tale.

"Did she die?" I asks. "The old woman, I mean."

"Why," says Jim, leaning over to lift a stove lid and spit in the fire, "I reckon she did."

"And did the Fool Killer come back then?"

"No, I reckon it was too late. Anyways, that ain't my point, George, and what I want to make sure is, did you get my point?"

"Well," I says, "I kinda see——"

"I want you to *know*, George! I want you to know the truth so's the truth can make you free. I want to save you. There's a fate worser than the Fool Killer by far, and it ain't hell, George, and it ain't the Devil."

"It ain't?" I says.

"No sirree!" says Jim. "Because just you keep in mind that whatever else the Devil may be, he's a *man*, George, he's of the male sex, whereas a good clean churchgoing woman can make him and hell both look like a mockery! That's the solemn warning I got to give to you, George. Just remember it, and watch your step from now on!"

"Yes, sir," I says. "I sure will try."

6

That night I slept bad, and I had terrible dreams.

I dreamt Jim come and told me that it was all a mistake about my folks being dead; seemed like they'd only moved away to another place, and now they had got on their feet again and wanted me to come to them right away. I felt so happy to hear it that I could of hollered; I couldn't wait to go where they was. So Jim told me how to go, and I set out. Only pretty soon it began to get dark; it seemed like I was in a woods, and I'd lost my way. Whichever way I'd look was trees without no path through them that I could see, so I figgered the best thing to do was set down and wait for morning. I set down under a big tree with my back against the trunk, and after I'd set there a while in the dark, I commenced to hear a sound. It was the sound of breath coming and going, but it was so loud I knowed it must have been the breath of something so huge that its throat would have been big enough to swallow me down in one gulp, and so near they wasn't any use me trying to run. I just set there, listening to the breathing getting louder and louder, nearer and nearer, until I was so scared I woke up . . . Only when I woke, the breathing didn't stop—I could still hear it, going in and out, loudern a old bellows, and near enough that I knew it was getting ready to jump, now; I could imagine it like a big cat sitting awful quiet, but gathering its feet together before it goes for a bird. I lay still as a stone with the sweat pouring off me, waiting, until Jim heaved a big sigh and turned over . . . It was him all the time, just giving a kind of odd snore.

I begun to shake, and then I turned round in the covers and snuggled down, and after a time I fell asleep once more. It seemed like I was back in the same dream then, only I'd got to the house where my folks was supposed to be. I knocked at the door, but nobody answered. I went round to the front, but still nobody came. I opened the door and went inside. They was nobody in the front parlor nor the back parlor nor the dining room nor the kitchen. I went upstairs, and it was all cobwebs and mildew and feathers spilling out of the bolsters where the mice had chewed, just like at Jim's house. I went to a window and looked outside. Everything seemed terrible still. Then all of a sudden I looked in the yard just below, and there was the Old Crab, staring up at me with eyes like red-hot darning needles, carrying a huge big chopper under her arm. She didn't say a word, just stood there staring that terrible stare until I was too scared to move. Then I begun to feel hot, and, looking down, I seen flames pouring out the first-story windows where the house was afire. It got hotter and hotter, and I knowed I'd soon fry like bacon, but if I jumped, the Old Crab would get me and chop through me like I was a segar . . .

Jim woke me from that one, shaking my shoulder. "Quit yelling," he says. "You been having a dream."

I *was* hot and throwed off the covers; then I sweat, and got cold. Finally I fell back to sleep and dreamed again. I dreamed Jim and me was setting in the kitchen like before we went to bed, and Jim was telling me a tale. A stove lid was off, and there wasn't no other light but the glow from the coals. "Don't you know who he is?" Jim says. "Don't you know?"

"No, sir," I says, "who is he?" knowing he meant the Fool Killer.

Jim didn't answer, but leaned down like he meant to pick up the whiskey jug, only when he come up, he had the chopper in his hand. I tried to yell, but my voice wouldn't work, and once more I was so scared it waked me.

This time I was like awake and asleep at the same time; I could see the dark room around me with the window graying up for dawn, and Jim there snoring in the dim light, only I was still scared of him like it was still the dream; I thought he was the Fool Killer for sure, and all his tales was only to put me off the track; I could see a kind of bump in his quilts, and I knew that was where the chopper lay; I wanted to get up and run, but I couldn't move at all, so I just stayed there shaking until finally I fell asleep once more.

This time, if I dreamed, I don't remember what; when I woke up I could tell by the light that it was late. Jim was up and gone—I couldn't see no bump in his pallet now, and anyway, I was full awake and knowed it had been a dream. My head ached and my face felt hot and swoll up so that I couldn't hardly open my eyes. I got up, put on my pants and shirt, and went in the kitchen. Jim wasn't there. I went out and pumped water on my head. That helped some. When I was drying, Jim come out of the privy.

"Good morning, slugabed," says he. "Hurry up and git yourself a bite, because this is the day I figure on going over to town to buy us some stores."

We went inside, and I had me a hunk of bread with molasses while Jim lifted up the loose board and took out the sock with his money in; I took our fishing poles to leave by the creek so's we could stop and fish on the way back, and we crossed through the yard to the woods behind the barn. Tom follered us for a time, his tail straight up in the air, zigzagging through the grass so businesslike it looked like he thought he was a hound dog. But finally he went off somewheres on his own, and I never seen that cat no more. Jim and me cut on through the woods towards where Jim said we'd come out on the main road.

It was a fine morning, with all the little new leaves out weak and green, and the sun shining through them. Birds was singing and Jim was whistling; a cottontail froze right in our path, but I didn't even have the gumption to chuck a stick at it. I still felt mighty queer; I kept stumbling over roots, and when we crossed the creek, I slipped off one of the steppingstones and wet my pants leg up to the knee. Then it seemed like the wetness made me shiver; my teeth begun to chatter, and if Jim had offered me a drink of whiskey then, be dogged if I wouldn't have took it, pledge or no. But he just hopped along ahead of me, whistling, or talking to hisself as usual, not expecting a answer.

After a time we come out of the woods, and, sure enough, there was the road. We took to it, and presently we passed a field of cows, a farmhouse, another, and then, from the crest of a rise, we seen the town. 'Twasn't but a few houses, down in the fold of a little valley, like some pebbles laying in the palm of a big green hand. It was a still day; smoke rose straight up from the chimneys like darning cotton hanging off a needle.

We walked down the hill and come to where the sidewalk begun, which somebody had just patched up with new yellow boards here and there, and then the hitching rail, with horses and wagons and a buggy or two tied up to it. Some folks passed who said Howdy to Jim, and one lady put her handkerchief up to her nose and pulled her skirts to one side as she went by. Then Jim says, "Well, here we are, boy," and we went in the store.

Well, if I didn't know it before, I oughta knowed I was sick then by the way when I went in I didn't even feel like looking at the candy jars. But I don't know if I'da been able to find them if I'd cared to, because standing there taking up just about all the space was left after the counters and the barrels and the stove and what not was about the hugest fattest lady I ever seen. She was so huge that I reckon them elephants in Africa I read about ain't much huger, and she filled that store so that the storekeeper looked like he'd got behind the counter so's to have it between him and her, the way you'd just as soon have the levee between you and the river when the water starts to rising.

"Now, Mr. Shinkle, I want three yards and a half of the blue, but I want you should show me ever inch of it as you measure it out, because blue fades so easy, and I don't want no——" she was saying, when all at once she turned and seen us. I reckon she caught a whiff of Jim, which called her attention. A expression come over her face like a mouse had run under her skirt, and I thought what a awful crash it would make if she was to faint away into one of them glass showcases. But I was feeling so fainty myself from it being close in there that I couldn't be sure any more was she really so big, or was I just kind of dreaming her so, on account of feeling so queer.

"Oh my land!" she says, when she taken a long look at us. "Oh my land, it's worse than a ghost—it's a living man! It's Uncle James Jelliman!"

"Howdy, Ova," says Jim, meek as Moses.

"Oh my Lord!" she cries, waving her hands. "If Aunt Myra Jelliman had lived to see this day!"

"The Lord giveth, Ova," says Jim, kind of beginning to back towards the door. "Come on, George, let's us go on down the street a while till the crowd clears out here."

"Oh no, you don't!" she says. "I'd never forgive myself! I'd never be able to meet Aunt Myra at the Judgment Seat and tell her I seen you looking so and never done a thing about it—and who's this here boy?"

"Boy?" says Jim. "Boy?" kinda looking around like he'd mislaid me. "Oh, George. Why, he's my nevvy from Maine. Yessir, come all the way down from Maine just to visit me. Nevvy on the Jelliman side, Ova. Great-nevvy, that is. Come on, George."

"Don't you move a inch!" she says. "You never had no folks in Maine, Uncle James. Step up here, boy!"

Seemed like there wasn't nothing else to do, so I done it. Looked like she got bigger as I got nearer. Looked like she was piling up over me like a thunderhead before a storm. She smelled, too, but not like Jim—like washing and ironing and starch and sweat and stoves. Before I could know what she was up to, she'd put out one of her fat little hands and laid it on my cheek. "Boy don't look right," she says. "Feels feverish, too."

And right then I felt my stomach turn round inside me and go the wrong way. I snaked round Jim and out the door; I run out and hung over the hitching rail, and it looked like every bite I'd had to eat since I'd run away come up and took leave of me.

What happened directly after that I can't tell you very clear, because I was kept too busy. Jim, he come out the store after me, with the fat lady after him, and the storekeeper after her— if I'd had time, I'd of felt terrible ashamed. Then somebody picked me up and put me in a buggy, holding me so's I could

33

hang my head out over the wheel; somebody took me out and carried me in a house which I guessed was the fat lady's, since she went to work and taken off my clothes without so much's a by-your-leave, washed me off some, and put me in a bed. I'd been sick so much I felt like I was turned inside out like a sock, yet I couldn't stop trying to turn right side out again. It was sure miserable. Somebody—her, I guess—give me a spoonful of something fiery, which I throwed back up, but she kept right at it until I held it down at last, and soon went to sleep.

THE FANSHAWES
7

When I waked up again, what I seen was a pitcher and a bowl standing on a washstand with blue roses painted on them. I didn't have the gumption to look no further; I just lay there staring until I seen the pitcher taken out of the bowl and water poured from it; a hand with a cloth dipped in the water and come out dripping; it squeezed the cloth and begun wiping my face with it, nice and easy. I blinked my eyes, and a voice says, "Well! I reckon you'll do now, praise the Lord!"

When I looked up, I seen it was the fat lady from the store, and even when I wasn't feeling so queer no more, she was about the fattest human being I ever seen. You heard the expression big as a house—well, she was big as a house with a piazza all the way round. She was all busted out in a sweat, like I later noticed she did for any little thing; it come out in her eyebrows, of which she practically didn't have none, and on her lip, like a little beady moustache.

"Now," she says, "you lay right still there, boy, and don't you budge a inch while I get you something to put in your stomach. Mind you don't jump around, because I ain't used to boys, and if you was to get ornery, I'd have to call Mr. Fanshawe, and he's got a terrible temper, Mr. Fanshawe has!"

I never said so, but I knowed I was lucky she hadn't told me I *had* to move, because I was feeling so washed out I don't know if I could of if I'd tried. Before I could say anything, though, she was gone out the room in a kind of slow hurry, like a wagonload of hay. While she was gone, I just laid there, not thinking of anything; presently she come back with a bowl of broth with some bread broke up in it, a spoon, and a napkin; she tied the napkin round my neck, pulled up a rocker, and begun to spoon-feed me like I was a infant. When I tasted that broth, I found out just how empty I was; 'twasn't no time until I got to the bottom of the bowl. Then she taken the napkin from around my neck, wiped off my face, and then her own face, which had got considerable damp from the exercise.

"Now, boy," she says, "I'm Miz Fanshawe. Miz Henry Fanshawe. I'm blood niece to Mr. James Jelliman's wife. That is, deceased wife. Now, boy, what's your name?"

"It's George Mellish, mam," I says.

"So 'tis," says she. "I recollect now, that's what Uncle James said. Now, boy—George—where you from?"

Up to then, I hadn't thought of nothing at all, or felt nothing either, except weak as a kitten and hungry as a bear. Now my stomach begun to kind of curl up around that broth. "Well," I says, "I ain't from any place much that you'd call any place, mam. I guess you couldn't say I was from any particular place at all."

"Don't talk nonsense," she says. "You know where you come from. Speak up and say."

"Why," I says, "I been visiting a spell over the way. That is, I been staying with Dir—with your uncle, Mr. James Jelliman, mam."

"Well, anyways, that's the truth, and a wonder it didn't kill you instead of leaving you only half dead. Now tell me the truth, boy, how long since you washed your ears?"

"Oh, months!" I says.

She threw up her hands. "I believe it! I believe it! Sick's you was, I been obliged to scrub you down from top to toe before I could bear to put you between my clean sheets, and they wasn't a spot on the length of you where I couldn't of planted potatoes in the dirt. And what have you been putting in your stomach since you was there?"

"Well, a little of everything, mam," I says, hoping we could go on this way for a while. "Dandelion greens and truck like that."

"Why, there's nothing better than a nice dish of dandelion greens!" she says, and I seen I said the wrong thing, only the Old Crab always used to say they'd run right through you. "Excepting it's too early for them by far. Now tell the truth, boy."

"Well, mam," I says, "Jim—Mr. Jelliman—he had a side of

smoked meat, and it was mostly that and some kind of greens once in a while, and bread, and molasses——"

"Bread!" she cries. "You mean to tell me Uncle James baked *bread!* Him? Now tell the truth, boy, it was so hard you could of paved a cistern with it—now ain't that so?"

Course, I'd never tried, but I wouldn't of been surprised on some of his batches. "That's right, mam."

"Capture him!" she says, and busts out in a sweat again. "Take a posse out there to the house and capture him like a lunatic—as who's to say he ain't? Oh, Mr. Fanshawe will never listen to me—he's *soft,* in spite of his temper, but if I put it right to the Ladies' Guild, don't you be too sure *they* wouldn't see it my way! We'll go out there in a body and tie him up and scrub him down! My own mother's sister's husband —I tell you, if I don't do something, I'll never be able to meet Aunt Myra in heaven!"

"He's a pretty dirty old feller," I says.

"Dirty!" she cries. "Dirt ain't the word! They ought to be something else to call it!" Then all at once she stopped, leaned forward, and looked at me sharp out of her little squoze-in eyes. "Here, boy," she says, "are you trying to distract me?"

"Oh no, *mam!*"

"I ain't used to boys, but I reckon they ain't *that* different from men. Now tell the truth, boy. What's your name?"

"George Mellish, like I said, mam."

"Oh lands, so you did! You got me all turned around. Now, George, where you from? That's what I want to know. Where you from and who's your folks?"

I looked up at the ceiling as sad as I knowed how, and I says, "I hope they're in heaven, mam."

"Oh!" she says. "Oh, they passed away! My, ain't that a shame! You poor motherless child! When was that, George?"

"I wasn't but a infant, mam," I says, as mournful as I could, but the minute it was out of my mouth, I knowed it was the wrong thing.

"Then what you been doing all this time? Who you lived with since?" she come right back at me.

I felt rightly cornered. I didn't know what to say. I thought about being sent back to the Old Crab and what a licking I'd get when I got there, and the tears begun to roll down my face. "I ain't nothing but a poor orphan child," I says, "been roaming the roads making my way in the world!" It just come to me like a idea, you might say. And then I seen the tears begin to roll

36

down *her* face, too, and before I knowed it, she snatched me over onto her till she like to smothered me, heaving and sobbing like a earthquake.

"Oh, I can't stand it!" she sobs. "I can't stand to think of it, you poor motherless lamb!" and she went on so until I got to feeling I was in a pretty bad fix just from listening to her, and hollered pretty loud myself; there was the two of us, bawling away, until finally she wipes her eyes and mine and says I'm to hush right up before I make myself sick again. Then she drawed the blinds, covered me up good, and I dropped off to sleep before she could even tell me to.

8

When I waked up again, I couldn't tell just what time of day it was on account of the blinds being down. What had waked me was the door creaking open. I looked towards it and seen a something sticking round the edge, not much higher than the knob. Whatever it was looked like a huge white butterfly to me, only shortly it come all the way in the room and turned out to be a hair ribbon on the top of a little girl. She come out from behind the door staring at me, and I stared right back at her. She couldn't of thought I was no more peculiar than I thought she was. She had hair so light it was almost white; little silver-rimmed specs that made her eyes look bigger than they was; she was skinny as a rail, and kind of knobbish at the joints. She had a doll almost as big as her under one arm, and a cushion under the other; first she come into the room, shut the door behind her, then she put the cushion on the rocker Miz Fanshawe had drawed up by me, and kind of eased herself up onto it, one side at a time, clutching at her doll all the while.

"I got a boil where I set down," was the first thing she said. Then she just set and looked at me a spell, and I guess I looked back at her.

"My papa says it's the meanness coming out, but my mama says it ain't neither, it's bad blood."

After that we set and looked some more.

"This is my dolly," she says then. "She come all the way from Paris, France."

I didn't know where that was at that time, so there wasn't nothing I could say to it.

"Ain't she beautiful? Her name's Secret."

I kind of nodded my head.

"My name is Blessing Angelina Fanshawe," the girl says, and then she slid off the chair—easy-like—put the doll down on the seat, and come over to me. "My mama named me that on account of having seven misses before she come to me. Blessing, like when you say the blessing." She leaned up closer to me, looking at me through the glasses of them little specs that made her eyes look as big as quarters of a dollar. "Some of the children at school calls me Blessy, and I just wanted to tell you that if *you* was to try it, I'd pick your eyes out with a fork."

I was blamed if I could think of a word to say.

"I ain't big enough to wrassle them down yet, but I reckon you're weak from being sick in bed. When I get bigger, I plan to pick *their* eyes out with a fork. Starting with that old Amy Shinkle. A sharp fork." She put her face right up to mine and stared at me hard. Then she backed off and cocked her head to one side. "Say," she says, "ain't you scared?"

"Of what?" says I.

"Of when I look at you."

"What should I be scared of you looking at me for?"

"The other children are."

"Well, I ain't."

"They get scared when I look at them through my glasses. I told them I got the evil eye. I can't beat up on them yet, but I can get them scared. Ain't you scared of anything?"

"Some things," I says.

"Like what?"

"Never you mind."

"Oh!" she says, and all of a sudden a extra foolish look come over her face (which wasn't too sensible looking to begin with, to my mind), she clasped her hands like she was going to say a prayer, and looked up towards the ceiling kind of cross-eyed. "I bet you really ain't scared of anything! I bet you're the bravest boy in the world and you can be my hee-ro and wrassle all the other children down so's I can beat up on them when they call me Blessy!"

"Wait a minute——" I says.

Then she stopped looking at the ceiling and went back and

eased up on the rocker again. "That is," she says in another kind of voice, "if you're here that long. Because you can fool my mama for a while, but you can't fool her forever. Sooner or later my mama gets to the bottom of things, you'll find out."

I wanted to tell her I didn't know what she was talking about, but I knowed very well that I did know, and I begun to feel pretty miserable, because, looking back on her ma, I could see how what this here girl said was likely true. I could see how Miz Fanshawe was the kind come back at you till she had you where she wanted you and all wore down and it wasn't no use to try no more. For all I knowed, she sent this here Blessing Angelina to see if she could get something out of me, too, but I was danged if I was going to give anything away to *her*.

"If it wasn't for me having a doll named Secret, there ain't no telling what she'd get out of *me*," she says then.

"How's that?"

"Whenever *I* got a secret, I tell it to my dolly right away, and then when Mama asks me, I haven't got it no more."

I was getting pretty tired of her nonsense, and I says, "That's crazy. It don't make no sense at all."

"No," she says, not getting mad at me like I thought she might. "It don't, but it works just the same."

"Then what do you say to your ma when she comes to ask?"

"Oh, I think of something."

"You mean you tell her lies."

"Well, I can't tell her my secrets when I ain't got them any more, can I? And with Mama, you have to say something— you surely do."

"You're just a common garden liar," I says, feeling more and more disgusted with her. "You don't need no doll at all."

Then she slid down again and come over to stare at me with those eyes that looked so big through the glasses and so little when you seen them plain, and I begun to see how them children was afraid of her—maybe she wouldn't of picked my eyes out with a fork, but I wouldn't of been surprised to have her bite a hunk out of me right then and there she looked so ferocious—puny or no.

"Don't you call me no liar!" she says. "I come here to help you, you—you runaway boy!"

Then I truly felt awful, for if that little spindling shrimp of a girl could see that I was running away just by looking at me, I couldn't doubt no more that sooner or later her ma would have the whole story out of me and send me back to the Old Crab before I could say Jack Robinson. She was a nasty-seeming little girl, all right, but hadn't nobody said they wanted to help me yet, so I says:

"All right, I take it back. Help me how?"

"Here's Secret," she says, and she taken the doll out the chair and set it by me on the bed. "You can tell it all to her so's Mama won't get nothing out of you."

"Oh pooh!" I says. "That ain't no good to me!"

"Don't you say no pooh to me, nor my doll neither, you slimy serpent!" she says, coming close again and snatching the doll under her arm. "You don't deserve no help! You deserve to lie in a old prison cell and starve! How do you know it won't be no good if you ain't tried?" And she turned her back on me and marched over to the door. When her hand was on the knob, she turned. "Besides," she says, "how you going to run away again without no clothes?"

Why, I hadn't had no chance to think of running away again, nor clothes neither, but when she said that it come to me plain as day that of course I'd have to run off from there, and I surely to goodness couldn't do it in the night-shirt I had on, which I figured must of belonged to her pa. "Wait!" I calls. "Don't go!"

"I'm going," she says. "Goodbye." But she didn't move.

"Listen," I says, "I didn't mean it."

"Didn't mean what?" she says, with her back still turned.

"Didn't mean you was a liar."

"Well, that don't make no difference. I am a liar, I suppose. What else didn't you mean?"

"Well—about your doll. I reckon she works all right—for you."

She turned around and come back a ways. "It'll work for you, too. Just you try."

"Well," I says, "all right. If you think so. But listen here. Do you know where my clothes is at?"

"Course, I know. My mama washed them, but they ain't dry yet."

"And where'd that be?"

"None of your beeswax," says she.

"Well, could you—would you get them for me?"

"Maybe."

"Maybe if what?"

"What'll you do for me?"

"Why," I says, "how would I know? I mean, I don't know what you want."

"Guess!" she says, looking at the carpet which she was scraping at with her shoe.

"I can't guess," I says. "I never seen you moren about a half a hour."

Then she heaves a sigh. "That's true," she says. "I reckon I'll have to tell it to Secret and she'll tell you."

Well, it seemed like a left-handed kind of a way to me, but I didn't care no more what she done, long as I got my clothes. She taken the doll's head up by her mouth and whispered to it. Then she taken the doll's face and put it by my ear. "Go on, tell him," she says, and then she waited a while.

Finally I says, "Secret ain't saying a word."

"She *ain't?*" she says, and blamed if she didn't look like she was getting ready to cry.

"I thought you said she never told no secrets anyhow," I says.

"Oh! I never thought! That's true."

"So maybe you better tell me yourself," I says.

"Oh, I *can't!*"

"If you don't, I don't know who will." I was beginning to give up on my clothes. I reckoned I'd have to get them some other way.

"All right," she says finally. "I'll have to tell. Only close your eyes."

So I closed my eyes and felt her climb up on the bed. Then she put her hand to my ear and whispered:

"I'm the only girl in Fifth ain't been kissed!"

When I opened my eyes, I could believe it. She was right on top of me there, with her skinny face and her bigger-than-natural eyes behind the specs, looking like something had just come out of a egg. I hesitated some, because, to tell you the truth, even if she hadn't been so homely-looking, I was in the same predicament as her—meaning I'd never kissed no girl before, neither, and furthermore, couldn't see nothing driving me to start in now. But then I thought of the Old Crab and my clothes and getting away from there, and I just shut my eyes and done it quick. It felt like I hit her somewheres around the nose.

The next thing I knowed, she was down off that bed like a streak of lightning, grabbed the doll and the cushion, and skedaddled out the door before I could hardly see she was gone.

41

9

After that, I laid there what seemed like a long spell without nothing happening or nobody coming near me. Outside I could hear sounds, like a rooster crowing and a dog barking and a woman's voice calling, "Char-*lee!*" somewheres far away. They was sounds inside the house, too, but not near ones. I must of dozed again; when I noticed next I could see the day was fading, in spite of the blinds being drawed, and I could hear footsteps coming near. Also I could feel them shaking the whole bed, so's I knowed it must be Miz Fanshawe on her way. Sure enough, the door opened, and there she was.

"Now, boy," she says, "here's Mr. Fanshawe come to talk to you while I'm getting supper. Speak up nice and don't tell him no lies, because Mr. Fanshawe's got a terrible temper! Step inside, Henry, and speak to the boy."

Well, sir, I hadn't seen hide nor hair of any living soul excepting herself when she opened that door, but then she come inside the room, and out from behind her come a kind of dried-up little feller with a bushy red mustache, thick eyebrows, like he'd growed another mustache on top of his eyes, and a bald head. "Howdy," he says, and I was some relieved to see he didn't look so terrible mean after all.

"Like I told you," says Miz Fanshawe to him, "this here boy's been staying out to Uncle James', and the wonder of it is he come out alive in time for me to snatch him back from the edge of the grave at all. His name's—oh Lord! ain't I forgot it again? I told you I wasn't used to boys!"

"It's George Mellish, mam," I told her once more.

"So 'tis, George. George. That's right. Well, Henry, this George here is a terrible liar—won't tell me a word about where he come from, when he's run off from somewheres as anyone can see, and his folks likely fretting themselves to prostration over him, the ungrateful limb! Mr. Fanshawe's the town

42

constable, George, and if you lie to him, you'll go to jail, sure as you're a foot high. Henry, show him your star!"

"Ain't got it on," says Mr. Fanshawe.

Then Miz Fanshawe throwed up her hands and busted into a sweat.

"Ain't got it on! I know what *that* means, Henry Fanshawe! You gone and lost your badge again! Last time I had to look for that badge I wrenched my back searching under the bed so's I couldn't even stoop to pick a pie in the oven for a week! Ain't my flesh affliction enough without you having no more consideration for me than to go losing your star? I'll vow you'd lose your head if it wasn't stuck on your neck, Henry Fansahwe, and the next time you come up for election, I'm blessed if I won't speak up to tell the folks how it is you look after town property! 'Tain't as if it was *your* star—come out of taxes, that star did——"

No telling how long she could of gone on—looked to me like she hadn't moren got started—but all to once, Mr. Fanshawe got even redder in the face than her; I seen his eyes kind of bug out and his eyebrows begun to wiggle like sixty.

"SHUT UP!" he roars, so loud I like to fell out of bed. And Miz Fanshawe did—shut up, that is—with her mouth just hanging open like a catfish. Then Mr. Fanshawe says real quiet, "I ain't lost it, Ova, it's right in my moustache cup like always, and if you don't believe me, go look for yourself."

She taken the corner of her apron and begun to wipe her face. "Shouting at me again!" she says. "Didn't I tell you he had a terrible temper, boy? Oh, you watch out for *him*—you ain't going to tell *him* no taradiddle like he was a poor weak woman." Then she shaken her finger at me and went off without another word.

When she was gone, Mr. Fanshawe shut the door and set down in the rocking chair. He fished a pipe out of his pants pocket, poked his finger in it, felt around like he was looking for his tobacco pouch, didn't find it, and set there sucking on the pipe anyway. It begun to sound kind of still to me. Finally he says, "Well, young man, what's this about running away?" and pulls his eyebrows down towards his nose.

Why, I thought, *I wouldn't much mind going to jail, if only they'd keep me there. There'd be folks to talk to, even if they wasn't but niggers, and they'd have to feed me. I never heard of nobody getting licked in jail, nor prayed over neither, though it's true I ain't had much experience in that line yet.* "I ain't running away, sir," I says.

43

"That's the first lie," says he.

But I was desperate, so I says, "I told Miz Fanshawe the same, and it's true. I just been staying over to Dirty—to Mr. James Jelliman's house, only I was took sick when we come to town."

Mr. Fanshawe begun to rock, and didn't say nothing for a while. I felt like I didn't mind the lying so much, but it was surely uncomfortable laying there waiting to lie.

"Staying out to Ova's Uncle James', was you?" he says finally. "Now there's a sly old bird."

Well, I was glad to tell the truth when I had the chance, so I answered, "He's a very nice old man. He was good to me."

"Oh yes, that's so," Mr. Fanshawe says, rocking away and pulling on the pipe so's it made a kind of whistling noise. "Uncle James always had a good heart." Then he didn't say nothing for a while. "Took you in, did he? Yessir, that's like Uncle James."

"Yes, sir, he took me in, and we had some good times together," I says, and I begun to think how we did have good times, and to miss old Jim, and to wish I was back to his house again.

Then all of a sudden Mr. Fanshawe stopped rocking, taken the pipe out of his mouth, and pointed the stem at me like the barrel of a pistol. "Taken you in, did he? Taken you in from where? Where'd you been? Where was you going?"

"B-been?" I says, kind of quavery. "G-going?" and I was good and scared. I knowed the Fool Killer must be standing with his ear cocked to hear what I'd answer next—that is, he would of if there had of been such a thing as a Fool Killer. "Well, sir, I was just kind of on my way, you might say. I was on a journey, that is. Heading West."

I was just about shaking, still being kind of weak, and all, and expecting him to jump on me that way again, but instead, he leaned back in the rocker and begun to rock and suck on the pipe.

"Going West, eh?" he says, and he looked up in the air the way a person does when he watches the smoke come out of a pipe, only his was cold. "That's the ticket! Used to dream about it myself when I was a youngun. Go out there and make me a pile and come back rich as Croesus. Make folks' eyes pop . . . Only I could never stand the thought of my poor old mother a-weeping and a-wailing for her little lost lamb. 'Oh, Henry,' she used to say to me, 'I couldn't *stand* it if you was to leave home!' And blamed if she wouldn't bust into tears just thinking about it! So, I never went . . . Ain't you never give a thought to them you left behind, George, wetting the pillow with a mother's tears?"

Well, I thought about the Old Crab, and I like to bust out laughing. "Hoh!" I says. "A lot *they* care! Reckon by this time they got some boy a lot handier than me!"

And with that he come down on the front of the rockers with a thump and pointed the pipe at me. "Who?" he says. "Who's they? Where they live? What town?"

I just looked at him, and I felt the sweat busting out on me like on Miz Fanshawe, only hers looked like it was warm, and mine was cold. I opened my mouth and shut it a few times, not knowing what in the world I was going to say, until all at once they was only one thing *to* say, and I said it quick as I could, which was:

"Excuse me, sir, I reckon I'm going to puke." And I did, without no further delay.

Well, Mr. Fanshawe he upset the rocker, but he jumped back in time, and I managed to hit the floor ruther than the bed-clothes. He yelled for Miz Fanshawe, and after that there was considerable flying around with mops and cloths and pails. Meantime I didn't have to do nothing but lay low and look puny —which weren't hard—feeling some ashamed, to be sure, but more relieved. And presently, when the cleaning up was done, Miz Fanshawe give me another teaspoon of the fiery medicine, washed my face, pulled up the covers, and told me to go to sleep right away.

10

I didn't go to sleep though. I felt kind of washed out and drifty, but not like sleeping no more.

I got to get away, I got to get away, I got to get away, my mind kept saying, like the wheels of a train of cars clicking over the ties, and then another part of it said, *How? Ho-ow?* like the whistle blowing, long and mournful. But the more I listened to what it was repeating, the less I could of answered it, just the way it is when you hear a train calling in the night and it seems to be asking you to do something or to go somewheres or trying to tell you something, only for the life of you, you can't make out what, or where, or how, and you wind up just laying in your bed, feeling sad for no reason you know.

Yes, I thought, *I run away all right, and I know what it was I run from.* Even when I'd think of some of the good times I used to have back there before I left—like sneaking off to go fishing, or swimming in the creek in summertime, or sliding down the back hill, after it had snowed, in a old dishpan which I hooked out of the loft, or finding a new batch of Tab's kittens in the barn before *she'd* had a chance to drownd them—even when I thought of them nice things while I was laying there feeling puny and strange and not knowing what to do next, it didn't come over me to say, *It weren't so bad,* or, *I reckon I could stand it some more.* All that ever come to me when I thought of turning back was: *I ain't going. I ain't and I won't. Wherever I'm heading, it ain't back there.*

I thought about Jim's, and I sure wouldn't of minded being there again—I'd of been glad. I thought about him and me setting with our feet in the oven of an evening, with Jim pulling on the jug and telling tales; I thought about him puttering about, losing things and looking for them, and of going fishing together, or ransacking about in his attic by myself—but, pshaw! I knowed that would be the first place the Fanshawes'd look for me if I was to ever get away—and like as not Miz Fanshawe'd catch hold of Jim and give him a terrible cleaning into the bargain, like she said.

I thought about heading West, too, but it surely did seem a terrible long ways away, and, to tell the truth, I didn't have too good a idea what it would be like when a person got to it. Injuns and gold and the Pacific Ocean and all like that . . . Only the more I thought on it, the less clear it seemed to get in my mind . . .

Yessir, all kinds of queer thoughts come to me as I was laying there, and all of them made me feel worse. I thought about how growed folks always looked like they knowed what they was up to without having no other growed folks to tell *them* what to do, and I wondered how a person got to be that way. It didn't look to me like growing taller and getting whiskers and talking like a man was going to fix *me* up all that different . . . And then I thought of Jim telling me about the Fool Killer—Lord, I knowed that weren't but a tale!—but somehow I couldn't get it out of my mind, that great big feller with the sharp chopper

46

with his eye peeled for when you'd act like a fool . . . Bad enough to *be* a fool without him looking over your shoulder ever minute . . . I knew it was foolishness thinking of him, yet it give me the shivers and I couldn't put it out of my head . . .

The house growed quieter and quieter until it seemed to me it must be late. I reckoned Fanshawes thought I was asleep and most likely had gone to bed themselves by now. I begun to feel hungry; I wondered if I got up real quiet could I find the kitchen, and maybe even my clothes. But I wasn't sure what time of night it was, or if they'd be in bed yet, so I thought I'd better wait some more.

I laid there listening to the noises. They was a cat fight outside, started sudden and then died away. A shutter was banging so I knowed the wind must be up. The house kind of creaked and settled—it *sounded* late all right. Then, all at once, I noticed a brightness beginning in the room; over by the door there come a kind of shine; I knowed by the way it looked that the door was moving open with a light behind, but I'd never heard the latch click, nor the hinges creak, nor footsteps outside, nor nothing at all. Next a candle come round the edge of the door; then, holding the candlestick a hand, and after that, just when I was getting prickles in my hair and gooseflesh down my back, Blessing Angelina come inside. She had a nightgown on, her hair done up in rags, and two little bitty candle flames flickering in the glasses of her specs. I guess I let out a sigh, feeling considerable relieved that it was only her—though if I hadn't seen her in the daylight before, I'd of thought *she* was a hant, for sure.

She had a big something under her arm which I couldn't make out what it was. She set it down on the seat of the rocker; next she put the candle down on the washstand, then she went back and closed the door as easy as she'd opened it. Finally she turned round and put her finger on her mouth.

"Ssh!" she says. "It is the witching hour!"

That took me funny, and I durn near asked her where was her broomstick, only I didn't want to make her mad.

"Now don't say nothing," she whispers, "but listen to me. My papa had a spat with my mama and started in to tearing up the turf about you and about how she was always taking in waifs and strays and how he was going to have you back where you come from before you could bat an eye, so you'd better get while the getting's good. I brought you your clothes, which is damp, so you'll probly catch your death, and some cake and pie and raisin cookies, which will probly turn your stomach after

47

you being sick the way you was, but they was all I could find. The next question is, do you want to eat now and run the risk of throwing it back up right away, or do you want to save it for later, but then you'll be weak as a cat without no nourishment and can't run if you're pursued?"

My heart had commenced to thud, but I didn't feel sick to my stomach no more. "I'll eat some and save the rest," I said.

She felt around in the bundle and got out the cookies, which she handed to me. "Don't eat them too fast or you'll get the colic," she ordered me, and though I could sure have wolfed them, I tried to chew slow.

When I was done, she says, "Now I'll turn my back while you put on your clothes." They was in the bundle, too; she pulled them out and handed them to me.

When she'd turned round, I skinned out of her pa's nightshirt and into my own things. They *was* damp all right, and my teeth begun to chatter. "All right," I says. "You can look now."

Then she taken something else off the seat of the chair. "Here," she says, handing it to me, "it's a old jacket I found in the ragbag where Mama won't miss it if it's gone—for a while, anyways. It'll keep you some warmer." I put it on, and was glad to have it. "And here's your food," she says, handing me a packet wrapped up in paper. "Probly my papa will put me in jail for aiding and 'betting a escaping criminal, but I don't mind."

I begun to feel kind of ashamed. She was such a ugly little old girl I couldn't hardly keep from laughing at her, but blamed if she hadn't been good to me. "Will you get licked?" I asked her.

She kind of put her hand around in back. "No," she says. "Probly not while I got the boil. And by the time it's gone, Papa will probly of forgot. But he might put me in jail. When Papa gets riled you can't tell at all."

"You been real good to me, Blessing Angelina, and I want to thank you," I says, though some way it come out hard. "I wish they would be something I could do for you some day."

The minute it was out of my mouth, I seen she was looking down at her feet, which was bare, and scraping on the carpet with one of them again, and I knowed what it was going to be, and knowed I *should* of knowed before I spoken, but it was too late now.

"Would you——" she says, sounding like she was choking to death, and I swallered a lump and says, "Sure." I set my packet down on the rocker, taken hold of her shoulders, and aimed

48

good this time. Looked like I was getting used to it—I hit her on the cheek right where I had in mind, and, to tell the truth, this time it didn't bother me no more than it would of to spit.

She put her hand on the spot and rubbed it—I couldn't tell if she was rubbing it off or rubbing it in—she looked up at the ceiling with her specs shining in the candlelight and says, "I reckon that'll show that Amy Shinkle!" Then she turns round and says, "Foller me!" and, taking up the candle, she led the way out the door.

11

We sneaked down the dark hall as quiet as mice, her showing me where to miss the creaky boards. Down the stairs we went and into what I reckoned was the front hall.

"Hold the candle," she says. "I got to unfasten the bolt. The back would of been easier, but my mama and papa sleeps in the bedroom over it."

I taken the candle and she unbolted the door. When she opened it, a big gust of wind come in and blew out the light. Outside, I seen the sky was full of big raggedy clouds chasing each other, but with stars between. Smelling the wind and knowing I was honest-to-goodness off and away, I felt gay all of a sudden, like I wanted to run and jump and didn't give a whoop whether I knowed where I was going or not.

"Yonder's the road," she says. "Back that way's where you come from—towards Great-Uncle James'. Don't go back there whatever you do, or they'll find you for sure. If I was you, I'd foller the road a piece until I come to the woods, and then cut through. They's catamounts and copperheads, probly, but I never heard of no bears, and out the other side you'll come to the turnpike, if you don't get lost on the way."

"All right," I says, "and thank you once more. I guess I'll be off then. I don't reckon we'll ever meet again, Blessing Angelina, so thank you for your kindness to me."

" 'Twas nothing," she says, tossing her head so's the curl rags bobbed. "I'd of done the same for a old stray hound dog."

I felt the wind a-blowing and seen the stars; I thought of all the adventures was waiting for me out there while she'd just be staying home with her pa and ma and all them children in school which she wasn't yet big enough to lick, and I felt kind of sorry for her as well as thankful. *It won't hurt me none,* I thought, so I taken a deep breath and says, "Would you care to have me kiss you again before I go?"

First she didn't say nothing but stood there staring at me, only it was too dark for me to see how. Then she put her hands on her hips and tossed her head like she was a horse with flies.

"I wouldn't of believed it," she says. "I certainly wasn't expecting any such of a thing, but it certainly 'pears like you're getting mushy on me. Now just get along out of here, you boy, before I say something I'll be sorry for!"

Well, I could of throwed the candlestick at her, but instead I handed it back nice and polite. "Goodbye, Blessy!" I says real plain, and skinned down the walk and out the gate before she even had time to think about picking my eyes out with a fork.

I stepped out on the road, and it was like starting in to run away all over again, only this time I didn't have no plan. But I reckoned the one I'd used before would be as good as any—find a depot or siding where they was a train standing, and ride the cars. Only I'd have to find one a good ways from this town in case Mr. Fanshawe'd be looking for me.

Fanshawes' house was out by the edge of town; beyond, I come to fields on both sides of the road, and nothing else but wind and clouds and stars. Ever now and then I looked back, but there wasn't a sign of nothing or no one, only the road stretching out behind me to where the town was already hid behind a rise. I walked along pretty smart for a while. Once I seen a horse with a white blaze on his face standing by a fence; I went over to rub his nose, but he tossed his head like Blessing Angelina done and galloped off the other way. I walked some more and begun to feel tuckered out. I thought I'd stop to rest and have me a bite—and then, didn't I remember I'd forgot the food?

Oh, I knowed where it was, just as plain—wrapped in a packet laying there on the seat of the rocker where I'd set it—and how come I forget it? It had went clean out of my head when I was kissing that fool girl!

I set down on a rock by the side of the road with the cold wind blowing round me, and the clouds racing over the stars above me, and I cussed ever nasty word I knowed, which was not enough. Then I set off down the road again, because they wasn't nothing else to do.

Over the way a piece, on my left, I could see where the dark woods begun, and while I wasn't anxious to go in among them trees with the copperheads and catamounts which Blessing Angelina had mentioned, I thought anyways they'd be some shelter from the wind there, and I could lay down and sleep a while at the edge of the trees and then cross through the woods in the morning after the sun rose.

So I climbed the fence and cut through the fields, but it looked like the more I walked, the further them woods was away, and the emptier and more weak in the knees I felt ever minute. Begun to seem to me like I was heading into them woods to lay down and die of starvation, and years later hunters or somebody would come upon my bones and say, "Why, this here looks like the skeleton of a boy!" . . . And I thought how I'd be nothing but a skull and rack of ribs by that time—if I wasn't scattered to the four winds by animals carrying off pieces of me—and it seemed like such a horrible ghostly thought that I got scared just thinking it, even if the skeleton I had in mind wasn't nobody's but my own.

The ground was rough where I was, and I was watching my step the best I could in the starlight so's not to fall; when I looked up to see was the woods any nearer, what met my eye give me a awful start after those thoughts of hants and dead bones and what not coming to me, for it was a light flickering among the tree trunks. What was a light doing in the woods at that time of the night? Couldn't be nothing but spirits, far as I could see—had it been somebody camping there, he'd of been asleep long ago and his fire down to coals, while this here one looked bright and moving.

Yet there's something cheerful in a light, even if twas to turn out to be a spirit's, and I kept on acrost the field towards it like it kind of drawed me. Then when I got close enough, I seen it *was* a fire all right; at the edge of the woods I got down on my belly and crept towards it, ducking and dodging behind the tree trunks so's my face wouldn't catch the light in case they was anybody there I wouldn't care to have see me. It was a good blaze and the smoke was coming my way; wasn't till I got up close and edged around to one side that I could see the man setting there by it, wide awake, late as it was, and not doing nothing but gaze into the fire.

I could see him good from where I was, and even with him setting down I could make out he was a tall lanky feller; he wore a coat you could see had been a soldier's by the brass buttons on it, but which was so faded out you couldn't tell had it once been blue or gray. His face was kind of long and crookedy, part covered over with sandy color beard, and running acrost his forehead from one eyebrow into his hair was a big angry-looking red scar, like he must of like to had his head busted open one time. But while I've seed fellers with scars that made them look some way odd or fierce or ornery, his didn't change the look of him no moren a scratch or a streak of berry juice he might of got walking through the woods. What give me a queer feeling about this feller's face that night, and made me scrounge back behind the tree trunk to make sure I couldn't be seed, wasn't the scar at all, but the way his eyes was set so deep back in his face that they wasn't nothing but shadows where you'd expect them to have been, except for once in a while a glint of light caught from the fire, like a possum's eyes when he runs acrost your path when you're carrying a lantern at night.

I had inched up pretty close, and I laid there watching him, setting with his hands clasped around his knees, staring into the fire out of them eyes you couldn't see. I lay still and he sat still; wasn't nothing to hear but the cracking of the fire and the wind blowing in the treetops; little by little I begun to feel quieted down. Then all at once, he begun to whistle, real low. He had a sweet, strong, trilly whistle; pretty soon he sounded it out loud. What he was whistling didn't sound like no song I knew, but it was tuneful—and sad! Why, that was the saddest song I ever *did* hear! It was such a mournful tune it made me begin to feel like a old hound dog which used to belong to the folks lived next to the church back home and couldn't keep from howling whenever the organ'd start to play. First the tears rolled down my face and I bit my lip to keep from making a noise, but shortly I begun to sob, big hiccuppy kind of sobs I couldn't no more stop than breathing. Lickings wasn't in it with that tune for making me bawl!

First off I sobbed quiet, but I kept getting louder and couldn't help it until all at once the feller broke off whistling. He jerked his head round, and called out sharp, "Who's there?" jumping to his feet. It like to scared the life out of me; for a minute I could hold my breath and be quiet. Then up come another sob, like a big bubble busting through me; before I could get up to run, or move any way at all, he taken two giant steps to the tree I was behind, reached round it, and collared me. "Come out of there, you!" he says, and then, when he'd drug me round the tree by the scruff of the neck like I was a cat, he says, "Why, 'tain't nothing but a boy!" and begun to laugh.

The tears was still running down my face; I wiped off my nose on the sleeve of my jacket. Then he stopped laughing and bent down, looking at me out of them eyes was set back in caves so's I still couldn't see them, even close up, when his back was to the fire. "Who sent you here?" he says, sharp and ugly.

"S-sent me?" I says. "Ain't nobody sent me."

"Then what you doing out here in the woods in the middle of the night? How come you ain't in bed at home? What's your name? Where you come from?"

Looked like them questions was the straw that busted my back. Great God A-mighty, wasn't they nobody couldn't stick his nose in my business? Where you from, where you going, go here, go there—I tell you, it looked to me like niggers was better off than children which hadn't never had no war fit to set *them* free! I took to bawling worse than ever then, and at the same time yelling at him and even kicking and hitting out with my fists.

"Who you think you are, anyway?" I yells. "Asking me who I am or where I'm from! What did I ever ask *you,* I'd like to know? If you think you'll send me back, you got yourself another think coming, because I ain't going and I ain't going to tell, and I'll jump in a pond and drownd myself if you try to make me!" And I flailed out like a crazy man, hitting him a crack on the arm.

He stepped back at first, looking kind of surprised, and the next thing I knowed, he had wrapped his long arms round me and picked me up like I was a baby. All I could think was that he meant to drop me in the fire, or hold me over it anyways, and I squirmed and hollered like sixty, but instead, he managed to set down on the ground with me in his lap.

"You're cold," he says, real quiet, and, reaching round into the dark behind him, he pulled up a blanket and throwed it round me as good as he could with me carrying on like I was having the fits. When he had me wrapped up, I couldn't thrash about so good any more, and besides he held his arms around me hard.

"Ssh!" was all he said. Ever minute or so, "Ssh!" And presently I begun to quieten, what with being tired, and him setting so still but holding me fast against his chest, where I could hear his heart thumping and feel his breath going in and out, steady and even . . . The next thing I knowed I had fell asleep.

MILO BOGARDUS
12

When I woken up next morning, the first thing I seen was him, hunkered down by the fire, holding a green stick with a fish on it over the coals. He raised up his head just then, but when he seen I was awake, he didn't smile or nothing, just give me a look, which was the first time I seen his eyes plain. They was mighty nigh as odd in daytime as they was at night, but in a different way, being very light-looking for human eyes—more like a goat's or a cat's, only gray, and set back deep in them caves, like, under his forehead.

I set up and rubbed my face. I knowed it was kind of late from the way the sun come down through the leaves and made the fire look pale. I throwed back the blanket had been round me and got up. He kept right on looking at me, just turning the fish a little to keep it browning even, and never saying a word. It begun to seem odd not talking, so I spoken up.

"You give me your cover," I says. "I'm much obliged."

He didn't make no answer, just kept on turning the fish, with the juice from it dripping and sizzling in the fire.

"I hope you wasn't cold," says I.

He shaken his head, and pointed to another blanket laying folded up neat on the ground with a canvas knapsack by it. I taken the one I slept in and laid it on top. Then he picked up a plantain leaf he had ready on the ground by him, pulled the fish off the stick with it, and held it out to me.

"Ain't you having any?" I says.

"I already et," says he.

So I taken the fish, squatted down like him, ate as good as I could without no dish or nothing, and thrown the skin and bones in the fire. I ought to said *thank you,* I thought when I was halfway through, but seemed like it was too late then. It sounded stiller and stiller in them woods without neither one of us saying a word; I had to kind of clear my throat before I could get my voice out to say:

"Do you know is there a spring or creek anywheres near that I could get me a drink at?"

He pointed off through the trees like he was a deef-and-dumb, and I got up and set off in the direction he pointed in, like I was another. Sure enough, down a slope I come to a stream. I reckoned he must of caught the fish there, for I could see a plenty of them, and cress, too, growing on the bottom, the water was so clear. I stayed there a time washing the grease off my face, taking a drink, and watching the fish swim by.

I could go right on, I told myself, *and never go back to where he is at all. 'Tain't as if it looked like he'd miss my company.* But that didn't seem right to me neither . . . *Wouldn't cost him nothing to open his mouth and say a few words,* thinks I . . . I set there a spell longer, recollecting the night before; how first off he frightened me, and then he give me his blanket and all, and was good to me. Finally I says to myself, *Well, maybe he taken offense at how I carried on. I expect I ought to face up to it and tell him I'm sorry I acted so* . . . With that, I got up and headed back for the clearing.

He was still setting where I left him, but he had got out a pipe to smoke, which smelled good. I stopped a minute when I seen him, give a swaller, then I marched right up to him and held out my hand.

"My name is George Mellish," I says, "and I'm on my way West. I reckon I cut up pretty foolish last night, and I come to ask your pardon."

He turned his head, looked at me, looked at my hand, and for a minute I thought he was going to go on setting there never saying nothing at all, which if he had, then I wouldn't of known *what* to do. But right away—only real slow and easy, like he was a tall tree growing before your very eyes—he stood up, put out his hand, and taken mine . . . My, he *was* tall, too!

"Howdy, George," he says. "Set down. I been figuring all the morning, getting ready to say the same to you."

"Same as what?" says I, feeling considerable easier. He hunkered down again, and so did I.

"Ask *your* pardon, too."

"Oh, say!" I says. "What for?"

"Last night," he says, and taken a draw on his pipe, "I come at you rough. I asked you questions wasn't none of my business. I asked you who you was, where you come from, and where you was going. In reply, you hit me a lick. Now, when I stopped to think on it afterwards, I recalled how I been asked the same question and made the same answer—punched the feller in the nose, that is to say. I wouldn't of asked a growed man his personal business no moren I'd expect him to ask me, was he a stranger, and I got no right to ask you just because you're a boy. I apologize."

"Oh, that's all right!" I says. But I couldn't help feeling kind of leary of was he maybe working round to asking me all over again.

"Yessir," he says, staring up at the tobacco smoke, "last night I was wrong. You was wrong some, but I was wronger. I had some reasons, but they ain't the point. I hadn't no right to treat you so." He stopped and pulled on the pipe once more. Then he went on. "Growed folks often does make mistakes. When you ain't growed, you don't know it's so; seems to you like they always know what they're about, which is why growed folks seems kind of odd to children so much of the time."

Then he stopped again, like it was time for me to say something, but since I couldn't deny it was so, it seemed more polite to keep still.

"Well, never mind," he says then. "It's over now. We'll forget it—and since you told me your name, fair and square, I'll tell you mine, good as I can. They call me Milo Bogardus, but that ain't my true name, I'll tell you right away."

"It ain't?" I says.

"Nosir," he says. "It was a name took off a dead feller and give to me."

"It was?" says I.

He pointed to the scar on his forehead. "It all come about in the war. When I got this here, it knocked me so I couldn't remember nothing which had ever happened in my life before, or even my own name, so when the feller in the bed next to me died, the folks in the hospital just taken his name and give it to me for mine. He was a bachelor without no kin, and anyways, many times there's two fellers with the same name, so I figgered it was no harm."

Up to now, I had been holding my fire, not wanting to be the one to get the questions to going again, but with that, I was too curious to bear it no more, and I asks, "Was you wounded in battle?"

So they told me," he says. "I never knowed. They picked me up and carried me back with the clothes all tore off me by the blast of a shell so's I never even known which side I was on. 'Twas a Union hospital, though."

"Couldn't you remember no fighting or nothing?"

He shaken his head. "Not a blamed thing."

"Nor anything before—not your ma nor pa nor where you come from nor nothing at all?"

He shaken his head again.

"Well," says I, "I surely never heard of such a thing! How *can* a person forget everything so?"

"*I* couldn't tell you," says he. "Often enough I wondered myself. I been over it again and again—all they is that I *can* remember: how it was when I woken up in the hospital, and from then on. I used to think that if I'd turn it over enough, some more would come to me. But it never did. Tell you what, George. If you want to go along with me a ways, I'll tell it to you—much as I can."

"Yes, *sir!*" says I. "I'd surely admire to hear!"

13

So Milo thrown dirt on the fire to put it out; he taken the knapsack and one blanket and give me t'other to carry; we was just about to set out when all to once a thought struck me.

"Hold on a minute," I says, "which way you heading?"

"Out t'other side of the woods," he answers.

"Oh," says I, fetching up a sigh, "*that's* all right." Then I wondered should I of said it, and would he ask me why I cared, and start with the questions again, even if 'twas in a polite way, but he never—just cut on through the trees like he knowed where he was going, and, sure enough, 'twasn't long before we come out on a trail. I follered along behind for a time until the trees got further apart; he waited up for me there, and we went along side by side.

"Now," he says, looking straight out ahead of him like he wasn't talking to me at all, "I'll tell you how it was.

"On account of what happened to me, I'm a man has got no history. Like I was born full growed. Or, no, it's more like I was never bore of woman at all, but come straight from God's hand, a finished man, but unknowing as a infant. That's how it was when I came to in that hospital.

"The first thing I knowed, when I knowed anything at all, was pain. Didn't seem like it was just in my head then, but like it was all around everwheres in me and about me. 'Twasn't even just in my body. 'Twas in my bed and my pillow and my covers and the air I breathed, even. That was to begin with.

"Then, gradual, I come to feel how pain was just in my head. 'Twas like two armies in there, trying to push the sides apart. And I begun to see and hear, sights and sounds and moving, and they was pain, too. Just pain was all the meaning they had to me. I'd hear water pouring, or a spoon chinking on a dish, or a groan, or words, or see a person pass in front of a window so's the light changed, and I'd know it, feel it, but not know what it was except pain.

"After a long time, the pain let up some, and things begun to come together in a meaning, like when God made the world, only slower. I seen I was in a great long room with white windows. I felt heat beating down from the roof. They was rows of beds and pallets to the right and left and acrost from me, with men and women moving back and forth among them. Sometimes a person stopping by my bed to tend me would say words, but I couldn't yet make out what they meant.

"And the next thing was that in amongst my pain come joy, because when I could look at things and recognize them for what they was, it was like whatever I seen was a miracle—and I mean everthing—not just the sun and stars come in the window, or water when I was dry, or sleep when I was tired, but the dirty bandages and the slop jars and the flies lit on the faces of them too weak to brush them away, too. The way I thought it out since, at that time I hadn't no knowledge of good or evil—'twas all wiped away—so all God's works was good to me, and wondrous thoughts come to my mind, though I couldn't speak them; all I wanted to do was praise God, not just for His flowers and birds and fresh air and loving-kindness, but for dirt and sorrow and dying far from home amongst strangers, too . . . Sometimes I'd try to sing out some kind of hymns from joy, the way I'd have to groan from pain others, yet I'd scarcely of knowed I was doing either one if it wasn't for how fellers begun to yell at me from their beds to hush up. They'd never bother me much if I'd cry from the pain, but when I'd sing out from joy, they'd cuss at me, and even throw things. Yet at that time the pain and the joy was all mixed up with one another to me, like they wasn't two things but the same."

Milo stopped talking, and we walked along quiet through the woods a piece. The sun was real warm where it come through the trees, and everthing smelled like spring . . . The way Milo talked made you feel like you was right there in that hospital with him in spite of it all sounding so strange; when he left off talking, I taken a deep breath like I'd come out of doors from inside. After a time, I says:

"I never had no pains made me feel joyful that way. The time I busted my arm, or when I had the earache, all *I* ever did feel was purely miserable."

It looked like he never heard me; he just kept staring on ahead like I wasn't there. Then, when I was about to give up on hearing some more, he begun again.

"Oh yes!" he says. "They was joy and they was pain. It looked like I was the only one took so with joy, but they was pain for all. Men and women went among the beds in that room trying to stop the pain, like a line of foolish children joins hands to try to stop the tide of the mighty ocean. But the pain come and come, like the tide. They couldn't stop it. Then it would go back, leaving some drowned in the flood and others washed up from the ebb. I could feel it coming and going in me like waves, the pain and the joy, the pain and the joy—but the tide was going out; I was healing up so's the pain was leaving me, and the joy, too, only neither one all the way.

"That was when I begun to understand words and to say them, and the folks there asked me my name. But I couldn't remember that, nor nothing else which had gone before, no matter how much they asked me. So when the feller in the bed next to mine died, they give me his name so's to have something to call me by.

"When I was strong enough to get up, I begun to go about helping the nurses, carrying food and slop jars and learning to change bandages. Sometimes my head would start to hurting again, so bad I'd have to go back to bed and everthing would be black for a while. And it was around that time when I begun to have the dreams, sometimes with parts of them which was like memories, but never clear to me when I woke up again. All I could hold onto out of them was that some was of men with black faces, jumping and shouting and running; laying down on their backs to load their rifles, jumping up to shoot them, then falling down again with half their heads shot away—and noise, terrible noise, so loud it woken me every time; while others was quiet dreams, like folks whispering outside the door, with me laying in the dark trying to hear what they said, only never catching anything clear except things like: *Watch out! Danger!* or *Beware!* And I'd wake up from them sweating, knowing for sure I had enemies somewheres, somehow, for some reason I'd never know.

"Other times still, I'd hear God's voice in the night, plain as a human's, telling me how ever man in that room was my brother. He given me the proof of His words, too, for when I begun to move around tending to them sicker than me, I found out I had been give a gift, which was to take away pain. Sometimes I could do it with a look, or sometimes by the touch of my hand. Sometimes the pain would pass out of the other feller through me and go away; others it would get into my head and I would have to keep it there. I never known how it was I done it, but they all seen it was so; the nurses would wake me up at night and ask me to come when somebody was took bad; they was one doctor hated my power and scoffed at it, but they was another would always call for me to be by when he knowed he must hurt a man. It was him wanted to send me to a hospital in the city for more learning—maybe be a doctor, too—but when I thought about it, the voices come in my dreams and warned me —in that terrible teasing way so's I couldn't but half hear them —that strange cities and strange houses was the places of my enemies.

"But finally the pain and the joy, and God's voice, too, begun fading away. Oh, they come back sometimes, but not so often, and not so clear . . . They said I was getting better, but they's times I ain't so sure. They's times I could weep in the night for them things I knowed . . . And at the same time, it seemed like my power to ease pain was fading, too. Seemed like it wouldn't work for me ever time or right away like at first it used to. It begun working better in the quiet of the night, when folks wasn't talking or moving about; I seen, too, that it wasn't the same for every man any more—some it eased, but others it left no better than they was. Finally I found out it was different according to who was nearby. They was one woman come in to nurse ever day who talked loud and walked heavy and took a thing away too quick when you handed it to her. I seen how it was no use for me even to try if she was there. Her or that doctor—him that mocked at me.

"And lastly, when I looked at the men and women around me —the sick and the wounded and those caring for them—I come to see good and bad amongst them, and I knowed that I was once more like one had ate of the fruit of the tree."

14

We come out of the woods then, and Milo stopped talking. The sun was most as hot as summer, and the birds was singing everwheres. We stood still, looking round. We was on the brow of a rise, looking down on a valley with a stream running at the bottom and another ridge beyond.

After a while I says, "Ain't it warm?"

First he acted like he didn't hear me—just stood there looking ahead. Next he turned and looked at me like I was a tree or a stone or something and he was thinking of something else. Lastly, I seen his eyes change, like as if his face was a house with the door closed, but then it opened up and a feller stood there saying, *Why, howdy, come right inside!*

"Less go swimming!" he says.

Swimming! 'Twasn't moren the middle of March! I'd never in my life heared a growed person think of such a thing!

"Yes, *sir!*" says I.

With that, he give me a tap on the shoulder, like last tag, and set off running down the hill, them long legs of his scissoring off three yards at a time, it looked like; me after him, fast as I could go, but falling down halfway and rolling the rest, just for the fun of it. By the time I'd catched up with him, he had his pants off and the buttons of his shirt undone; by the time I was out of my clothes, he was in the water, splashing it back at me. I run in and begun splashing him, too. Great Day but that creek was cold! Took your breath away and made you holler at the same time! 'Twasn't more than knee deep anywheres, and I don't know that I'd of had the gumption to get wet all over but for slipping on the stones and falling down. I come up gasping and whooping; Milo, he dipped in apurpose, but come out again fast, too; then I run up on the bank and he run after me; he chased me a time, and could of catched me easy, of course, but let me get away; then we done different tricks—he turned a real good cartwheel; I did some somersets, forwards and backwards, and 'tempted to stand on my hands but tumbled over;

after that we run halfway up the hill and rolled down again. By that time we was pretty warm and out of breath; we laid down on the bank in the sun and just rested there with our hands under our heads, feeling grand.

After a time, I says, "Can't you remember no battles or fighting at all?"

"Some," he says. "I was stretcher bearer for a time after I got out the hospital."

"Like what?" I says. "I'd surely like to hear about that."

But he says, "No. I'm too peaceful now."

Then we was quiet a time.

"Did you ever see the ocean?" says I.

"Yes," says he.

"I never did. What's it like?"

"Green," he says, "and gray and blue and purple and black and still and calm and fearful and quiet and all the different things you can think of different times. You could look at it forever and never get tired, the way it never stops changing."

"Was it the Atlantic or the Pacific you seen?"

"The Atlantic," he says, "and the Gulf of Mexico."

"I aim to see the Pacific when I get West," I says. "But the main reason I'm going out there is prospecting for gold. Jim—that's a feller I knowed—he says if I watch my step and don't act too foolish, I might make my pile and be a rich man."

"Why?" says Milo.

"Why?" says I. "Why—because—well, wouldn't it be great to strike it rich and build you a great mansion and have a carriage and pair and a diamond ring and—and all?"

"No," says he.

"Wouldn't you like to have a thousand dollars and go in the store and just say *Give me that!*—whatever it was you wanted?"

"No," says he.

"Well," I says, "what would *you* like, then?"

"I like to eat when I'm hungry, sleep when I'm tired, talk to folks when I feel like it and not when I don't, and travel about seeing the world."

I couldn't think of nothing to say. 'Twas him spoke next, after a time. He says:

"I can feel the grass growing under me."

I couldn't, so I says, "I can feel a piss-ant walking round my big toe."

"I can feel the sun and the air and the earth all over me," he says. "Men don't go naked enough."

"Injuns do," I says, "but they ain't but heathens."

Then we was both quiet again until all of a sudden, without knowing I was going to say it, or expecting it or nothing, I says, "I run away."

"Is that so?" says he.

"But it wasn't my own folks I run from. It was folks had took me in after my own folks died."

"Well," he says, "I reckon you had your reasons."

"I was running away again when I met up with you," I says. "From the constable in whatever that town was back yonder. He said he was going to put me in jail if I didn't tell where I come from, but I never."

He picked a blade of grass and begun chewing on it.

Then I rolled over on my belly so's I could see better what his face looked like, and I says, "Milo, did you ever hear tell of the Fool Killer?"

"No," he says, turning his head towards me, "what's that?"

So I set out to try to tell it the way Jim told me: how the Fool Killer was a great giant, like, and if you wasn't careful he'd come and chop you for a fool. And I told about Jim, how I come to meet up with him, and the good times we had and all, and the kind of feller he was, not believing in cleaning his house or hisself or having no women round, and how he was always chattering along so's you couldn't just tell what was a tale and what not . . . I got to talking and it looked like I couldn't hardly stop; I told him all I'd told Jim and more, too: about the Old Crab and the Old Man, about the Fanshawes and Blessing Angelina, and, in the end, it looked like the notion I wanted to fetch up with was this: did he think what I'd done and how I'd acted and all sounded like I was something extra of a fool?

"Who ain't?" he says.

"Laws, I ain't but twelve years old!" says I. "I ain't had the experience to judge. But, of course, I forgot—maybe you don't remember even as much as me."

"Yes," he says. "There's some truth in that—one way of looking at it, you might say I weren't but five-six years old. But I traveled a lot in them years. I seen a lot of men. And I been off to myself, too, thinking of what I seen. I've pondered on the peculiar things I seen folks do—foolish you could call them. 'Pears to me like fools is what God made us, so like as not there's some sense to being a fool if we could come to look at it the right way."

"Well," says I, "I wish I knowed what the right way was. Oh, it don't bother me none when I'm going swimming or turning somersets or even laying here talking to you. But when I'm alone and feeling any way low in my mind, I get to wondering if I ain't about the biggest fool ever lived, and—well, don't matter what I tell myself, I just *feel* like there might be some kind of a something like a Fool Killer coming after me . . . You know what put me in mind of it? Them dreams you told of, when you heard the voices outside the door saying *Danger* and *Beware* so that was how you knowed you had enemies."

"Oh, that," he says, and rolled his head away so's I couldn't see his whole face no more.

Then my heart started in to pound and I felt the cold ground under me which the frost wasn't yet out of in spite of the sun, and I got the goose pimples down my back.

"Milo," I says, "Milo, there ain't no real Fool Killer, is they?"

He didn't answer for a minute; then he turned his head back and looked at me. "I don't know, George," he says. "How could I answer you they was no such thing just because I never seen him nor heard tell of him? There is many things on earth which men don't know and ain't meant to and never will. So we all got fears, both of them things which we know and of them which we don't and can't."

I couldn't stand laying there no more. "I'm cold," I says. "I think I'll put on my clothes."

"All right," he says, and got up, too. "It's time we was on our way." And he begun putting his clothes on same as me.

But even when I was dressed, I was so cold my teeth begun to chatter, sun, clothes, and all. Milo heard it and looked at me —I seen he noticed, but he didn't say nothing, just picked up the knapsack and blanket and loaded them on. I felt so bad I begun to wonder if maybe the Old Crab was right about a person being bound to catch his death going swimming before the first of June and maybe I had caught mine. Then, when I had t'other blanket over my shoulder all ready to go, Milo put out his hand and laid it on my arm; he just left it there, and shortly my teeth stopped chattering. I could feel the feel of him, quiet and steady going right through me, like when he held me the night before—it was like his hand was talking to me, along with his mouth.

"Listen a minute, George," he says. "How'd it be if you and me was to travel along together, since we seem to be pretty good company, and we're heading the same way?"

Right away the warm come back in me, and I felt like a weight rolled off my shoulders, or like I'd most slipped off the barn roof but catched myself and been saved. My eyes begun to water, and I had to take a minute before I says:

"That'd be fine, Milo! I'd like that fine!"

15

So that was how we begun to travel together, Milo and me. We was together—oh, about a month, I'd calculate, traveling in a general westerly way, before—well, before what I'm going to tell you about. My first notion was like I had before: that we'd go on to the next town and ride the cars. But Milo says:

"What's your hurry? Less take it easy and see a thing or two."

And, thinking it over, I didn't feel like I was in no particlar rush, leastways not now I had somebody to walk with and talk with and all . . . Also, I kind of give up on the idea of prospecting for gold and striking a vein and becoming a rich man, after talking with Milo some more. What's there in being rich? Money don't buy much besides troubles, and anyways, you don't need it to have you a good time. I surely did have some good times with Milo!

We just moseyed along, mostly traveling by shanks' mare, but hitching a ride in a wagon sometimes; following the roads until we come to a town, then cutting round the by-ways so's not to pass through. We fished and we hunted—though we didn't have no gun, Milo could stun a rabbit or a squirrel with a stone near as square as a rifle shot, and teached me so I got pretty handy at it, too. Then sometimes when we'd come to a house, we'd go up to the door and ask was they a job of work for us; that time of year they was usually something to help out on— lambing or plowing or planting—and if it was anything to do with animals, Milo surely had a knack for that. I seen him born twin calves from a cow had been suffering so long the farmer was getting ready to shoot the poor old bossy, and he was great on smithing, too—he could shoe the skittishest horse like one-two-three. Me, I'd just stand by, keeping my eye peeled for whatever way I could help Milo; afterwards, he'd always say to me, "Why, you're as handy as a pocket in a shirt!" and I'd feel proud.

When we was done with whatever it was, the folks would ask us in to eat, and we'd stuff ourselves on woman-cooked food; in the evening we'd set around jawing with them, or singing songs, or telling tales. Then they'd offer to put us up for the night, but Milo would always say, *Thank you kindly, no,* and we would sleep out in our blankets somewheres, or, if it was raining, in the barn. Milo never told no one else why that was, but he told me: because strange houses and strange cities was the places of his enemies. Sometimes the children would gather round me and ask questions about where we come from, where we was going, where we slept nights, wasn't we cold in winter, didn't I have to go to school, and all like that. But however kind folks acted, I was just as close-mouthed as I knowed how, for Milo had trusted me with his true story, which he never told to no other, like I had trusted him with mine, and I wasn't taking no risk of betraying him to his enemies when he didn't even know hisself who they might be.

That was how we went along, hunting and fishing and stopping off to lend folks a hand, taking our time, but moving westward right along, through countryside looked like it was afire from all the blooming that time of year—first the red-bud, then the dogwood, then the apple trees, then the lilacs—pink and red and white and purple, with all the rest that bright new green. When the weather was warm, we'd take off our clothes and swim in a creek like that first time, though the water was still cold as ice everwheres; then we'd come out yelling like Injuns, running about doing tricks to get dry, and falling down and laughing fit to bust when we was tired. Milo wasn't much of a one for laughing—he'd smile or get a look like a chuckle in his eye—but when he felt good from running or swimming or so, you could see the laugh coming in him like coffee boiling up in the pot, until he'd trip me, or knock me down, and the two of us would lay on the ground bare-naked, laughing at nothing much of anything until the tears was streaming down.

And also I seen Milo cry, which was when he had one of his spells from being wounded in the head, only I didn't figure out that was what it was till afterwards. And even if I'd knowed it at the time, I don't know that it would of helped any. Oh, I hate to remember it, for it was a terrible dark time! I don't like to hear it when a growed man cries! And to hear it in the woods at night, with him the only one I had to count on at all!

I can recall how the day before it happened was a gray sort of day which kept looking like it was fixing to rain but never did, and we was tramping along a road through open country with not a house in sight for miles.

Most times if I'd ask Milo a question, he'd take trouble and answer it good, even though he might not answer it right away, but wait until he'd thought it over for a while. This day, all he'd say if I'd ask something, or speak, was *Yes* or *No* or *Maybe,* until finally I says to him:

"Did I do something wrong, Milo? Are you mad with me?"

But he only give me another short *No.*

"What's the matter?" I says. "I just know they's something wrong!"

"They're near," he says then. "I can tell it. They're near."

"Who's near, Milo?"

And he says, "My enemies."

We was on the top of a hill; I turned and looked back; then I looked in front of us and all around. "Ain't nothing but open country for miles and not a soul in sight," I says. "You must be mistook. It can't be."

"They're near," he says. "I feel it. I always can."

Well, I reckoned he'd know more about it than I would, but I didn't see how it could be. We went along without saying nothing for a time, and then a idea come to me. The more I thought of it, the less I seen what the answer was, so finally I says:

"Milo, if all men is your brothers, how come some of them is your enemies?"

He turned so sharp, and his eyes was so big and angry looking that I thought for a minute he was getting ready to hit me, or collar me, anyways, like he done that first night. I seen him open his mouth and shut it without saying nothing. Then he says:

"Cain and Abel was brothers, wasn't they?"

And he turned his head and begun walking so fast I had to run to keep up with him; neither of us said nothing until finally I had to call out:

"Wait up, Milo, I'm plumb out of breath!"

He walked slower after, but he still never said a word, and we went along like that until the light begun to go; just then we was passing a woods; without a word Milo turned into it off the road. I follered him until he stopped and dropped the knapsack and blanket on the ground; I put down my blanket, too, and set about gathering wood for a fire. I heared water running nearby, which didn't surprise me none, for Milo was like a animal for smelling out a creek or spring even from far away. I taken the canvas bucket out of the knapsack and followed the sound down a bank to the stream, but when I come back with it filled, Milo hadn't started the fire, or even built it—he was just setting on the ground by the pile of wood I'd brought, hugging his knees and staring into nothing. So I hung the bucket on a limb and built the fire; I got out the tinder box and struck a light; pretty soon they was a good blaze going; I taken the hunk of side meat out of the knapsack, found me a green stick, cut us a couple of strips, and begun cooking it over the fire. When it was done, I held the stick out to Milo, but he just pushed it away from him like it was a branch of a tree got in his way when he was walking through the woods. I wasn't so terrible hungry myself, but I swallered mine, taken a drink, and went in the bushes; when I come back, Milo was wrapped in his blanket, laying on the ground with his eyes closed, so I got my blanket and rolled up, too.

"Goodnight, Milo," I says, but he never even answered me. I felt pretty blue; however, we'd walked a far piece that day, and I fell asleep soon.

It was the sound of his sobbing woken me. I couldn't of been asleep long, because I seen the glow from the coals of our fire still shining up red on the undersides of the leaves. I raised up, and in the light I seen Milo laying on his back holding his head between his hands like he had to do that to keep it from falling apart, and at the same time rolling it back and forth, from side to side, and sobbing.

"Milo!" I says. "Milo, what is it?"

But they was no answer, only that terrible, dry, deep sobbing. I shaken off my blanket and went to kneel down by his side. I taken hold of his arm to try to stop that awful rolling of his head, for they was something about it scared me worse than the sobs—but it was like he never felt me lay hand on him.

The creek we was camped by was down a steep bank. I run to it, slipping and sliding so when I got to the bottom I fell in the water up to my knees. I taken off my shirt, wet it, and scrambled up the bank again. I tried to prize his hands away from his head, but I couldn't, so I laid it over his face, hands and all. Then he grabbed it and pressed it to his forehead, changing from the sobbing to little moans, like it felt good to him.

All that night he was that way, and the next day and the next night. They wasn't hardly anything I could do but go back and forth from the creek, wetting the shirt and a old bandana I found in his pocket. A night and a day and a night he lay there sobbing and moaning, until I fell asleep finally, because I couldn't stay awake no more. When I woke, they was no more sound, and that scared me worst of all.

I jumped to my feet before my eyes was hardly open and looked around the camp. It was just daylight, with the birds all going like a thousand fiddlers tuning up. All I could see was his blanket, laying in a heap, not rolled neat the way he always left it. I couldn't think where to look, but I run down towards the creek. And I let my breath out like a groan when I seen him kneeling by the stream below me, dipping up water to drink from his hands.

"Milo!" I says, and he heared me, and turned. His eyes was the brightest I ever seen them that day; they shined like stars back in their dark caves.

"Oh, Milo," I says, "I thought you was going to die!" And I begun to shiver all over, so hard I had to set down.

"Oh no!" he says, shaking his head, "I wasn't nowheres near dead, George. I seen God!"

"You did?" I says, just setting there on the ground shivering. "Oh, Milo, what did He look like?"

"Like a light," says he. "Nothing but one big shine. The brightest anyone ever seen!"

"Is that all?"

" 'Twas a reglar glory, George!"

Then I flopped over on my belly, wrapped my arms round my head, and begun to bawl.

And all I could think of, even when Milo come and taken hold of me, and soothed me and comforted me, was what a terrible disappointment it was that that was all there would be to it if a person was to see God.

16

Yes, that was one terrible time. It passed, though. Milo didn't seem no different at all afterwards, but for a long while, I would wake up in the night with a jump, listening for I don't know what, and in the day, I taken a habit I was ashamed of, yet it looked like I couldn't keep from it, which was this: sometimes when Milo and me was walking along not saying much, I'd manage to drop back a step and grab hold of something on him where he couldn't feel it—like the tail of his soldier coat, or the flap of his knapsack. It never come over me to do that way when we was talking, but when we was going along kind of still, thinking our own thoughts, it looked like once in a while I just had to take ahold of him somewheres, like if you hold out your finger to a mooley calf, he can't keep from sucking on it. Once I did it so's he felt me, and turned to see what was up, but I made up I'd been brushing a ladybug off him. And that was odd to me, too, because by then I'd of thought I could of told anything in the world to Milo and not feel ashamed . . . Anyways, I got over that habit by and by, and waking up at night, too, and everthing was just the same—Milo and me going along together, having a fine time.

Besides that, Milo taught me many things—I don't mean like things in school, but things a person could have a good time learning, or have some use for. Like that about hitting a rabbit with a stone, or how to make a willow whistle, or where to pick yarbs and make a ointment to rub on a cow's udder when her teats was sore, or how to tell the good mushrooms from the pizen kind, or how to turn a cartwheel. Them things was easy enough, even when they taken me a time; then they was other kinds was harder—talking kind of things more than the doing kind. Some of them I understood pretty good, but others I couldn't puzzle out, even thinking of them afterwards.

Like lots of times when Milo'd get to talking about God. 'Tweren't like the Old Man. When Milo talked about God, you'd of thought He was just about human, and interesting, too. But it 'peared like Milo was agin religion that was the reglar kind.

Milo used to say how preachers was always telling you man is born in sin, but Milo, he didn't cotton to that idea at all. To his notion, we was all God's creatures, come from His hand the way He made us—good, that is—only cities and clothes and houses and railroad trains and things like that all come between us and God and caused us to kind of lose track of Him. And the ones should be helping folks find their way back to God— preachers, that is—is so busy telling them how sinful they are, and how they're going to hell if they don't repent, that folks get tangled up worse than ever, till, first thing you know, they get to thinking they ain't worth the powder to blow thesselves up with, and, *next* thing you know, danged if they ain't out having a war, *trying* to blow thesselves up! While all the time, if they only knowed it, why all folks would have to do is reach out their hand to touch God!

Well, naturally I can't say it as good as Milo did, because a lot of it was too deep for me. At the same time, it used to make me feel kind of easy in my mind when he'd go on about that, even if I wouldn't understand everthing he'd say. It was a relief to think maybe I hadn't ought to feel like a miserable sinner all the time, which I hadn't never been able to do as much as I thought I probly ought to of, anyhow . . .

And then, I'd think of the Old Man, thumping down to ask for God's mercy ten-fifteen times a day—even times he had the rheumatiz, too—and it'd make me laugh to split my sides thinking how if he'd only knowed it, he had it anyways, all the time! Milo said I should feel sorry for him stead of laughing, because it wasn't no joke to *him,* and I don't reckon it was, at that, but I couldn't help laughing just the same.

Sometimes Milo would get to talking about children and growed folks, and how they wasn't as different as growed folks mostly give children to believe; I'd tell different things about when I lived with the Old Crab and the Old Man; sometimes Milo would say I'd been right and them wrong, or sometimes that he thought I'd been mistook, and if I'd been older or hadn't lost my temper, I'd of seed it another way. Sometimes he'd bring me round to his way of thinking and sometimes not, but whichever it was, wouldn't neither one of us mind. Because, like Milo always says, we was true friends and good companions, and I knowed one thing: whatever Milo told me, whether I understood it or not, agreed with it or not, it wasn't no lie. Milo never lied to me—not even to josh me, or to make a long story short, or to tell a interesting tale, or any way at all. Whatever he told to me was true as he'd of told to a growed man, and some things he told me he never told to no one else at all. Like that about his enemies. He trusted me, like I did him.

One time when we was laying in our blankets at night, with our feet towards the fire, looking up at the stars, Milo was talking about when he was in the hospital after he got his wound, the way he often did. He was took there after a great battle, and when he come to hisself they told him it was a Union hospital, but he never did find out which side it was he'd been fighting on, Union or Secesh, on account of having forgot everthing, and having the uniform blowed right off his back, too. Anyways, this night I'm telling of, he was saying how when he realized he'd never be sure had the men around him been his comrades or enemies, that was when the idea come to him that, from that day on, them fellers and all the other men he'd ever see would be his brothers. Well, I told that before. But this night, he said he didn't just mean manner-of-speaking brothers, but real brothers. Because, he says, if a man didn't know his own name, or where he come from, or who his folks was, how could he ever know who was his brother and who not?

But, like I said, the way Milo talked was often kind of over my head. I recollect I answered him:

"If a man was your brother, though, I reckon he'd remember *you*, Milo. I mean, if *he* wasn't shot in the head and forgot everthing, too, which would be kind of unusual—having two in the same family hit in the same spot that way."

He didn't answer me for a minute, and I could hear him moving round in his blanket. Then he says:

"If *you* was my brother, *you* wouldn't know!"

"Why, why wouldn't I?" says I.

"Because you'd of been too little to remember it when I went off to war!" he says, rising up on one elbow to look at me, like he was kind of excited. "For all you know, you *could* be my brother!"

"Well, I wish I was," says I, "but I never had no big brother went to war. I wish I had of, all right. Maybe he'd of come back and got me instead of me being took in by *them* and having to run away and all. Unless *he* was wounded in the head and forgot everthing, of course. But, pshaw, Milo! everbody in town knowed my folks, and they never had no other younguns but me. I guess it's unusual a person would have a brother and not know it."

Then Milo shaken his head so them shaddery eyes of his which was always hard to see at night catched the firelight.

"You don't understand!" he says. "You don't understand!" And he twisted round and lay down again with his back to me so's I thought I must of made him mad, but I didn't know what more to say.

And now I'm sorry I answered him that way. I wish I'd said, *Why, sure, we could be brothers—how'd I know?* Or I wish I'd said, *Less be blood brothers and cut our fingers and sign a oath in blood!* Or anything, to let him know how I *felt* like brothers . . . Only I'd of thought he'd known that. Why, Milo was the first person I ever seen give me a idea of what it would feel like to have folks!

My own folks died when I weren't moren a year old. Neither of them had growed up in that town where I was born—my pa come there to work in the sawmill after he married my ma. Not being very old folks, I don't reckon they was expecting to die, but they taken the typhoid fever, like a lot of others did at the same time, and they was gone before anybody had time to ask them where their kin lived, or what did they want done with me. Maybe they hadn't no kin—maybe they was both orphans, too. Anyways, they wasn't nothing in their things to tell by, neither —and by the time I was old enough to hear about what happened to them, they wasn't even a tintype left for me to see what they looked like . . . 'Twas the Old Crab told me as much as I knowed about them, and about how her and the Old Man taken me in after they was dead . . . She'd tell it over again whenever she'd start in on how sharper than a rattlesnake's tooth is a ungrateful child . . . That was all, though—how they died, and how my pa's name was Tom, and my ma's Nancy. Sometimes when I was laying in bed at night, it used to seem to me like I had a kind of picture of what they looked like somewheres in my mind—but no sooner would I think it was coming to me than I'd go off to sleep . . .

So, things being the way they was, I never give much thought to folks until that night I met Milo, and then, the first thing he done was the thing made it come to my mind. Oh, I don't mean the way he collared me and pulled me out from behind that tree! That was only because I'd give him a start, like, when he heared me there, and Milo always had to be careful on account of knowing he had enemies. Then I was scared myself, to begin with, because of already feeling pretty spooky before I ever laid eyes on him; at first all I taken notice of was how he had a good grip on me so's I wasn't likely to get away. Still, even after he picked me up, I struggled and lashed around, hoping I'd twist loose by some freak of luck—and that was when, little by little, ever time I'd push up against his chest or buck out against his arms, I begun to feel something about him which was quieting and gentling along with being firm and fast.

"Ssh!" he kept saying to me. But he didn't mean *Hush your nonsense before I teach you to shut up!* He meant, *Hush now, ain't no reason to fret so!* and I could tell it just by the way he felt . . . All you got to do is watch how different fellers will handle a horse or dog to know how they got as many different ways of touching as they got of talking, and the way Milo held me that night—well, I remember thinking, before I fell to sleep while he had me there, *Why, this must be how a person's folks would feel!*

THE CAMP MEETING
17

One evening, Milo and me was going along a road a little before sundown, and I was walking backwards so's I could look at my shadder, which was all long and stretched out behind me, like winter underwear hanging on a line.

"Why you reckon folks has shadders?" I says.

"I never give it no thought," says Milo.

"Maybe it's like your soul or your spirit or so."

"Might be."

"Supposen a person was to lose his shadder—wouldn't that feel queer?"

"Maybe—or maybe he'd never even notice."

"That's true—and then one day he'd be going along like us now, and when he seen the other feller's shadder so long and spread out, all of a sudden he'd think, *Glory be, where's mine?* You reckon he'd start wondering was he dead and a ghost and never knowed it before, Milo?"

"I couldn't tell you," he says, "but I can tell you this: if you don't turn round and watch your step you're going to wonder how come you thought you was standing up when all to once you're setting down."

So I turned round, and when I did, I noticed a church steeple sticking out of a clump of trees down the road.

"Hey, Milo!" I says, "look yonder—we're coming to a town."

"Sure enough," says he, and right away we jumped the ditch and cut south through the fields. That was what we always done —stuck to the highways until we seen a steeple or a bunch of roofs and then found byways to go round, just like we never slept in no one's house, on account of Milo knowing that strange houses and strange cities was the places of his enemies.

We crossed a creek on a log, climbed a hill; when we come to the crest, we stopped. They was a wide valley with a grove of trees growing in it spread out below; and in amongst them trees was some kind of doings going on. Smoke was rising up like from campfires; they was horses and mules hobbled or tethered near the edge of the trees; you could hear folks' voices, a dog barking, and a baby crying.

"Why, what is it?" I says to Milo. "It's a odd place for a fair, but what else is all them folks there for? Come on, Milo, less go see!"

But he grabbed hold of my arm. "No," he says. "Less go round."

"Oh gee whillikers, why, Milo?" says I. "Don't it look kind of gay? I bet you we could get us a meal, too. I can smell chicken frying clear from here!" And I taken his sleeve and give it a pull, I had such a hankering to see what was going on.

"They's too many folks," he says.

"Why, that's just the thing of it!" says I, but then it come to me what was in his mind.

"It ain't a strange house," I says. "Nor yet a strange town."

And then I says, "But if you think we better, we can just as well go round."

And when he didn't say nothing, I told him, "Shucks, it don't matter, Milo. I already been to a fair."

He looked down at me then, first with his face all sober, then with his mouth turning into a smile amongst his beard.

"You really pine to see what's going on, don't you?" says he.

"Oh pshaw, not if you don't think we ought to, Milo!" says I.

"Well," he says, "you're right. 'Tain't a house and it ain't a town. Less go see what in tarnation it can be!" Then he give my arm a squeeze and let it go; we started off together down the hill.

When we come to the edge of the grove, a little bitty black and white dog with a curly tail run out and begun barking at us like we was breaking into a henhouse. He was so little and so sassy he made me laugh. "Howdy!" I says to him, and held out my hand for him to smell, but blamed if he didn't come flying at me and take a bite of my pants leg. I was so took by surprise I lost my balance and sat down.

Right away, a little old woman come busting through the trees, spry as a rabbit.

"Shep!" she hollers. "You, Shep! Ain't you shamed? Let go that poor little feller!"

I got up so's she could see I was most as big as her when I was on my feet, and I give my leg a kick to shake the dog loose. He started right in to barking again.

"Now shame on you!" says the old woman. "I'm purely mortified by your evil ways! You go right back under that wagon like I told you! Go right back, sir! You hear what I said?" She shaken her finger at him, but he never budged.

Then I seen a big heavy-set man with a black hat on his head and a bushy beard on his chin coming behind her.

"Ma!" he says. "You make more racket than that dog! Since when has he took to minding anybody? I told you he wouldn't stay if he wasn't tied!"

At that, the old woman swooped down and grabbed up the dog under her arm.

"He's 'titled to his freedom same as the rest of us!" she says. "He behaves real good when he ain't put off by something strange!"

"Well, take him back where he'll feel at home so's a body can hear hisself speak," says the man, for the dog was kicking and yapping under the old woman's arm all the while. So she switched him round like he was a baby and carried him off; meantime the man come up to Milo, holding out his hand which Milo taken and they shook.

"Solomon Arkwright's the name," says the man. "That weren't a very brotherly greeting."

"Milo Bogardus," says Milo. "No harm done."

"You just git here, Brother Bogardus?" says the man.

"That's right," says Milo.

"You're going to hear some powerful exhorting, I can tell you. You're going to thank the Lord for leading you along His paths to this place. This here your boy?"

"This here's my friend, George Mellish," says Milo.

"Howdy, George," says the man, holding out his hand to me, and I shaken with him, too.

"I reckon if you all just come, you'd like to sit down to some victuals with my ma and me before the evening preaching," says the man. "Ma's just about to take the pot off the fire, and there's a plenty."

I couldn't tell from his face was Milo fixing to say yes or no, so I given his coat a pull to let him know I was about starved. He looked at me, and then he says, "That's right kind of you, Mr. Arkwright, we'd be proud."

"Brother Arkwright, Brother Arkwright!" says the man. "We're all brethren and sistern here! Come right along with me!" We followed along after him through the trees.

When we come further into the grove, I could see there was even more to whatever it was there than it looked at first sight. The middle of the grove was cleared right out in a kind of square with logs laid in rows on the ground the length and breadth of it, and at one end a big platform, like, set up on posts. The clearing was empty except for two little tads not yet out of dresses having a good time swarming over the logs, but all around the edges of it, amongst the trees, bunches of folks was gathered around fires, cooking. Looked like each bunch of folks had a camp; some with tents, some with wagons covered with canvas over hoops, good as a tent, and some with just a tarpaulin throwed over the wagon sides for shelter. I seen crates of chickens setting on the ground here and there; they was one wagon with a cow tied to the tail gate, but it surely wasn't enough stock for it to be a market, and nothing about it looked like it was a fair.

Brother Arkwright and his ma had one of the reglar tents set up, and a board on stumps in front of it for a table with logs for seats alongside. When we got there, the old woman was dishing out stew in tin plates.

"I thought you'd bring em with you," she says. "Hurry up and set down, and if you want your food hot, Solomon, for mercy's sake don't pray too long!"

She set down by one plate, Brother Arkwright by another, and when Milo and me had put our traps on the ground, we set down, too. I was all ready to dig in when Brother Arkwright taken off his hat, folded his hands, shut his eyes, and begun to ask the blessing—and I seen what his ma had in mind. He went on so long it seemed to me he could of read off half the New Testament in the same time, what with the smell of that stew blowing my way, filling my mouth with spit and my belly with emptiness. I never waited for a Amen so long. But it come, finally, and we begun. Maybe we talked some, but as I recall it we mostly ate until we was done, then had some more, and when Shep come nosing between my knees, I sneaked a bit off my dish so he could have some, too.

"Thank you, mam," I says, when I finally pushed back my plate. "That surely was good."

"Why, I'm obliged to you, too," she says. "I forgot what a satisfaction it is to see a boy dive into your cooking." Then she reached down in the pocket of her dress, pulled out a clay pipe and tobacco bag, filled the pipe and lit it from the fire.

"Oh, Ma!" says Brother Arkwright when he seen what she was at.

"Now, Solomon!" says she. "You know I ain't been saved yet this trip, so let me take the good out of being backslidden long as I can!"

With that, a idea come to me. "Is all these folks here for a prayer meeting?" I asks.

"Why, they's more to it than a prayer meeting," says Brother Arkwright. "It's a camp meeting. Ain't you never seen one before?"

"No, sir," says I.

"Wasn't you aiming to come here, Brother Bogardus?"

"No," says Milo. "We're just travelers happened along."

"Are you saved?"

"No," says Milo, kind of short.

"I was once," says I, "but I was awful little, so I reckon I'm backslid by now." I was stretching a point, since all I ever done was stand up for Jesus in prayer meeting one time when I seen everbody else doing it and thought I ought to, too, besides being pretty tired of setting down. But I didn't want Brother Arkwright to think we was heathens, and Milo didn't look like he had much to say.

"Well, praise God He guided your footsteps this way!" says Brother Arkwright. "You'll hear some mighty fine preaching."

When Milo didn't say nothing, I says, "At prayer meetings we never had no preaching. Just hymns and folks getting up to testify."

"Well, sir, at camp meeting they's singing and testifying and preaching, too. We got three preachers spells one another, morning, afternoon, and evening for a solid week. You'll see many moved by the Spirit, here. Yessir, you'll see jerking and shouting and speaking in tongues—we had them all already. Say, you'd have a hard time to hold back from getting sanctified was you to want to!"

"What's all them things—jerking and shouting and speaking in tongues?" I asks.

But he only shaken his head. "God moves in mysterious ways His wonders to perform," he says. "You'll see. Yessir, you'd have to fight hard to keep from flying to His bosom!"

"Now *that's* the truth!" says his ma, taking her pipe outen her mouth. "You take me for a example. Ever year, reglar as the clock, Solomon's got to go to camp meeting to git hisself saved, and I got to drag my poor old bones after him. Why? Because if I wasn't to come along to keep my eye on him, first thing I know he'd come home married stead of saved. And once I'm here, I dassn't even give in and get saved myself until the last meeting. Why's that? Because if I was to let myself, I'd be too busy feeling sanctified to keep my eyes peeled, and first thing you know that fat Widder Perriman that's always rising to

78

testify about her sinful thoughts would take her mind off the preacher and go to work on Solomon. Nosir! I got to be careful to stay sinful till the very last day. Now Solomon, he gets saved ever meeting, to make sure it'll take."

"Oh, Ma!" says Brother Arkwright, like she hurt his feelings bad. "They's sin at camp meetings like everwheres else in the world, because the Devil's trying hard to get a foothold and spoil the Lord's work, but when did you ever see me carry on any such of a way?"

"Marriage *ain't* a sin," says his ma. "That's what's troubling me. Nosir, Solomon, I'm too old and too mean for grandchildren messing up my house and some strange woman underfoot in my kitchen. You can just wait till I'm dead and gone, since you waited this long. Here, young feller," she says, getting up and gathering the plates, "will you just take these dishes down to the creek yonder and wrench them off before the preaching begins?" and she handed them to me.

"Yes, mam," says I, taking the plates, and I headed off the way she shown me, and I seen others going, too.

Some ways off, I heard Milo's voice calling after me, and I stopped and turned. He was follering me; he caught up and put his hand on my shoulder. "Wash the plates," he says, "and I'll gather our things so's we can go."

"Go?" I says. "Oh, Milo, ain't we going to stay?"

"Ain't nothing to stay for but a lot of preaching and hymn singing."

"I ain't much on preaching, neither, but don't you like to sing hymns?"

"What's the matter with you?" he says, and he sounded mad. "You fixing to listen to what a sinner you are all the evening and then go up and get yourself saved?"

"Oh no!" says I. "It ain't that at all! It's only I never been to a camp meeting like this here. Don't you hanker to see all them odd things like he told about—jerking and shouting and all? And besides, it's interesting when folks gets up to testify different ways they sinned. Shucks, it wouldn't be like church, Milo! We can just get over by the edge of the clearing so we can sneak off through the woods any time. Oh, Milo, why don't you want to stay?"

I seen him open his mouth and shut it, like he was going to say something but didn't. Then he says, "Why do you?"

"Well," I says, "like I said, it sounds interesting and I never seen it. And then, we ain't been around any folks in a long time."

For a minute he was still. 'Twas most dark; when I looked at his face, his eyes was hid in shadder, back in their caves. Then he let go my shoulder.

"All right," he says. "Go wash them plates and come on back. We'll stay."

And he turned round and walked away from me.

18

They was other folks washing off their supper things up and down the stream bank, but I didn't get talking to none of them, only scrubbed the dishes off with sand and went back to Arkwright's camp. 'Twas just dark by then, and four big fires was lighted up at the corners of the clearing, blazing brighter than the ones folks had been cooking on. Just as I got near I heard a horn begun to blow and seen a feller walking round with a bugle. Brother Arkwright and Milo was getting up from the table as I ome; Miz Arkwright taken the plates from me and says:

"Go long with the menfolks. Preaching's about to start."

I follered after Milo and Brother Arkwright acrost the clear-in ; from all sides the folks was flocking in amongst the logs c d taking seats on them like church pews: women and girls on ne side, men and boys on tother, with a space down the middle or a aisle.

Up in front they was lighted pine knots set all round the platform; pretty soon I seen a tall skinny feller in a black suit climb up there and stand with his hands folded in front of him, the torchlight flickering on his face, looking round at the folks below. I reckoned he must be the preacher, which Brother Arkwright just then turned round to tell me he was.

'Twas Milo led the way amongst the logs with Brother Arkwright and me behind; he picked places way over by t'other edge of the clearing, and when we started to set down, he leaned acrost Brother Arkwright and says to me:

"Come set over here, George."

I knowed that was so's we could sneak away when we wanted

without nobody noticing, so I climbed over and set by Milo on the end.

When the seats got filled up, I couldn't see around me so good, but I knowed everone must be there when folks stood up and begun to sing, kind of weak and out of step with one another to begin with, then good and loud. 'Twas "Jerusalem, My Happy Home," and I joined in, too, but when I taken a look at Milo, I seen he weren't singing, and the thought went through my mind how when he got his wound and forgot everthing, he probly forgot all the hymns and such he used to know, too, only then I recalled how he'd told that he used to sing hymns in the hospital, and I thought I'd try to remember to ask him about that later on . . . Ain't it odd the way a person can be thinking one thing and doing another?

After we sung the Amen, we set down, and a couple of folks in different parts of the clearing shouted out, "Hallelujah!" and, "Glory to the Lamb!" but the preacher spread out his two arms like a big skinny black crow to show he wanted them to be quiet, and soon it was still enough to hear the fires cracking. Then he begun to preach, and though he didn't look much bigger round than a fence post, the voice come out of him would of put a bull's beller to shame.

"WATCHMAN!" he calls out, so loud I like to jumped out of my seat, "WHAT OF THE NIGHT?"

Then he stopped, looking all around the lot of us setting there below him, and my ears rung, hearing the stillness after his voice. But when he begun again, he was so quiet you'd never of guessed he was the same man, yet you could understand him plain.

"The sun has set," he says. "The darkness gathers. The peaceful creatures of the day has give way to the savage prowlers of the night: the lion, the tiger, the wolf, the bear, and the painter."

Where I was sitting on the end of a log they wasn't any camp nearby—I looked right out in the trees where it wasn't nothing but black, and it made me edge over towards Milo. Not but what I didn't know they was no lions and tigers in them parts.

"When night falls, brothers and sisters, Satan calls them man-eaters forth from their lairs and lets 'em loose in the peaceful forest, where their evil deeds is covered under the cloak of darkness. But that ain't all. When night falls, the Devil whistles out the beasts of passion and carnal sin from their kennel, like a feller letting loose a pack of hounds, and he follers

81

after em, breathing fire from his nostrils and lashing his angry tail, waiting till they pick up the scent and tree thesselves some sinners."

He stopped again, and I heared a screech owl, like a ghost laughing back in the woods somewheres; then nothing but folks breathing around me, and the crackling of the fires.

"SINNERS!" he hollers all of a sudden, so I jumped again. "How did you sleep last night? Did you wake from the nightmares and wonder was these campfires shining before your bewildered eyes the fires of hell, waiting to swaller you? Did you hear rustlings and whisperings in the bushes and wonder was they the hounds of hell a-smelling after you? Did you hear the sound of footsteps sneaking nearer and wonder was they the Evil One a-coming, coming, coming for YOU?"

I moved up closer still to Milo, and he put his arm in back of me. Behind me, I heared a voice give a kind of groan and say, "Oh Lord, ain't it the truth!" but real low.

"When sinners wakes in the night, shivering and crying out with fear, it ain't in them to know which way their help lies. Sinners reaches for the bowie knife under their pillow or the shotgun leaning by the door. But they ain't no bullet can drop the Devil in his tracks! They ain't no knife can pierce the hairy hides of the beasts of sin! When the Devil sees the sinner thinking to save hisself by his own strength, he laughs, knowing he'll get him for sure! Or sinners piles up silver and gold to build them mansions and bolts the doors with bolts of iron. They drinks liquor and smokes tobacco and pleasures their flesh, thinking to forget the day of reckoning at hand. Then when he sees the sinner wallering in depravity, the Devil claps his hands for joy. But when the Lord of Hosts sees the sinner thinking to save hisself by his own arrogance and worldly vanities, He is mighty wrathful, and cries out, *Fool! Fool!* But the sinner don't heed."

I felt Milo take his arm out from behind me and I looked at him to try to catch his eye, but he was staring at the preacher like he didn't want to miss a word. I was glad it didn't look like he was getting ready to leave, because I was powerful interested, in spite of having the shivers down my spine. The Old Man and the Old Crab used to carry on about sin enough, and so did the preacher back there, but not as if 'twas lions and tigers rampaging about like they'd escaped from a circus menagerie.

"THE SINNER DON'T HEED." he yells out loud once more. "THE SINNER DON'T HEAR! His ears is deaf, his eyes is blind to the voice of the Lord! His mouth is buttoned up tight's a pocketbook, so's he can't pray! The Devil's got him before and behind! He's got sin to the right of him, sin to the left of him; in front of him yawns the gates of hell; behind him comes the tramp of Satan's tread, nearer and nearer still!

"The sinner can't move, brothers and sisters! He's bound by sin. He's deaf because his ears is stopped with it and dumb because his mouth is shut with it. That's why we got to SHOUT to him, brothers and sisters! We got to PRAY for him! We got to TESTIFY to the goodness of the Lord! Oh, who's going to rise up and speak out his heart?"

First nobody budged; then, a few rows in front of where we was, a little stooped-over old feller got up, taken off his hat, and turned round.

"Brothers and sisters," he says in a quavery voice, "I'm one of them sinners can't sleep, like the Reverend says. Ever night of my life the gas on my stomach wakes me and I toss and turn, in Satan's power. I ask all to pray for me, because I ain't yet saved."

Different places around the clearing, folks called out, "Hear him, Lord!" or, "Take it to Jesus!" or, "Lay it on the altar, brother!"

Over on the women's side, a great red-faced lady got up, and, speaking out most as loud as the preacher, she says, "Oh, brothers and sisters, I want you to know the Reverend Spotts has got God in his heart and can't speak what ain't true! I want to testify to you how the night is the time when the Devil wrestles us down and gets us on our back, all right! But when I'm laying wakeful and them hideous thoughts comes to me—when I think Satan has got me by the throat and ain't going to let me go— then I call on my Redeemer to help me, and He washes me as white as snow!"

I heared Brother Arkwright whisper to Milo, "That there's the Widder Perriman—Ma don't do her justice; she's a fine religious woman." But Milo didn't even nod.

Then Brother Arkwright, he stood up and looked around. "Brothers and sisters," he says, "for many years I prayed for my salvation. But the Lord held back the light until one day, when I was pulling on a cheroot, I heared a voice say, 'Solomon, lay down that smoke!' And I never touched tobacco since, nei-

83

ther to smoke nor to chaw, and I had God's light in my heart, shining brighter ever day. I *know* my Redeemer liveth!"

Then he set down, and I couldn't tell was it the preacher started it or who, but somebody struck up a sort of dreary tune which we all got up and joined in.

> Think of what your Savior bore,
> In the gloomy garden,
> Sweating blood at every pore
> To procure thy pardon;
> See him stretched upon the wood,
> Bleeding, grieving, crying,
> Suffering all the wrath of God,
> Groaning, gasping, dying.

I never did care much for that one, and it sounded worse than I ever heard it out there in the woods in the dark.

After that, the preacher come right up to the edge of the platform and spread out his arms again. When everybody had set down and was quiet, he says:

"Brothers and sisters, who is it we got gathered together here in this grove, seeking salvation at this here meeting? I *think* some of them is Baptists; they *may* be more of Methodists; they *could* be a few Presbyterians, but oh, brothers and sisters, what I *know* we got here in plenty is SINNERS!

"We got sinners here has come for nothing but to mock and scoff and have thesself a good time in carnal pleasures. We got sinners come to make a profit on selling trash and gewgaws amongst the faithful. And then, we got sinners come here because, in the midst of their sinning, they heared the voice of the Lord, crying out, 'Fool, fool, why doest thou not forsake all and foller after me?' Yes, brothers and sisters, them sinners heared his voice like thunder, and it turned their blood to water and their bones to ice; they shaken in their beds and groaned in agony, for they knowed the Lord was angry with them, yet they knowed not which way to turn."

I begun to wish he wouldn't mention that about the Lord saying to sinners they was also fools. That was the first time it ever struck me foolishness was anything to do with sinning, and, between that and him talking about hearing footsteps and waking in the night, it all took me back to them awful dreams I had at Jim's about the Fool Killer. Supposen, after all, the Fool Killer was like a story in the Bible that meant something different from what it said, like when God disguised Himself in a pillar of fire or a burning bush or so? Suppose 'twas God and not the Fool Killer at all it meant in the tale?

"Them sinners knows the Lord their God is just," he was saying, "and they know how He sees all. So they know they got no hope of deceiving, and they quake with terror—it seems to them that if 'twasn't for hell, they might as well lay down and die.

"And then—then there comes to them, faint and feeble through the clouds of wickedness, the words they heared at their mother's knee—JESUS SAVES!

"What is the hope of them sinners, brothers and sisters? Who is it leads them to places of holiness like this here, sometimes they don't even thesselves know why? Oh, it is Jesus Christ, their Redeemer! Oh, it is Him going to plead for mercy for them at God's judgment seat! He sitteth upon the right hand of God and He whispers in His Father's ear, 'Let him off this time, Lord, he won't do it no more!' And God heeds His only begotten son, and listens to Him, and mingles His mercy with His justice.

"And what does Jesus ask of them sinners in return? He don't ask no burnt offerings nor heathen sacrifices. He don't ask they should go off in the desert and become hermits for His Name's sake. All he asks is for them to truly repent their evil ways. All he asks is for them to get down on their knees and ask pardon for what they done wrong, to bow their stiff necks under the yoke of His perfect love and know what wretched weak creatures they are and how they got no help nor hope but Him. All He asks is for them to open their hearts so's His holy spirit can enter there."

Right then, a woman near the center of the clearing shot up in the air with a whoop like she'd sat on a rattler, then fell down in the aisle like she was dead or fainted away. I craned my neck and tried to see, but it looked to me like they just left her laying there. The preacher went right on.

"Yes, a sinner is a filthy critter, abominable in the sight of the Lord. He's weak and he's vicious and he's ornery, so it's only by a miracle they's any hope for him at all. But they *was* that miracle, brothers and sisters, when the Lord gave His only begotten son for them very miserable worms! And when the night is darkest and the evil beasts prowls near, Jesus comes to save us with comfort and forgiveness if we will truly repent. He is our comrade in battle and our brother by our side. He'll take us in His arms and soothe our fears. Oh, Glory to the Lamb!"

With that, all the folks rose and begun to sing:

85

Glory to the Lamb! Glory to the Lamb!
The world is overcome by the blood of the Lamb!
Glory to the Lamb! Glory to the Lamb!

over and over, until some begun to clap, and then all taken it
up, and to stamp their feet, too. Then I seen a feller run out to
the edge of the clearing, climb on a stump, and begin to twitch
back and forth, first leaning over his knees like he had the
cramps, then bending back to where he was most inside out
until finally he fell off the stump and lay on the ground thrash-
ing around. They was more yelping begun on the women's side,
like a bunch of wild Injuns going it over there, and it was a time
before the preacher could yell loud enough to make folks quiet
down. I felt all strung up like a banjo myself—that hymn was a
regular ripsnorter when it got to going—and I would of got up
and give a holler myself if I'd of dast.

"HE SAVES!" the preacher kept yelling at the top of his
voice—and, as I said, he had a good loud one. "HE SAVES!"
until finally most folks set down and was quiet, except for somebody yelling, "Oh, glory!" or, "Amen!" now and then.

"JESUS SAVES!" he hollered again, his voice ringing round the
clearing like a clapper in a bell now that it was still.

"Come unto me all ye who are heavy laden, He says. Though
your sins be as scarlet they shall be white as snow; though they
be red like crimson they shall be as wool. It ain't me that's asking you, brothers and sisters, it's HIM! Come forward and
repent! Bend your knees and bow your heads—He'll take you
in His arms, filthy and disgusting though you may be! Without
Him, you ain't but a louse crawling on the coat of the world!
Repent and give up to Him and He'll make you shine like one of
the stars of the firmament; He'll stand between you and the
Devil; He'll ask His Father's forgiveness for you! Oh, once
you're Jesus' slave, you'll know what it is to be free!"

'Twas harder to hear that last part of what he said, because
ever minute more folks was beginning to moan or call out.
"Amen!" they'd cry, and, "Praise His name!" Back behind me,
I heared a voice talking real excited in some kind of gibberish,
or maybe it was Greek or Eyetalian or so, and, twisting round,
I seen another feller climbed on a stump acting like he was giving a sermon in that funny lingo, not paying the preacher nor
nobody else no mind. Then a woman over on tother side give
out a high scream, and calls out, "I'm coming, Lord! Stretch
out Thy arms and catch me—I'm on my way!" and she went

stumbling down the aisle with her arms out and knelt down in front of the platform.

When the preacher seen her, he called out, "Oh, brothers and sisters, here is one sinner come to give up to her Lord! Which one is coming next to find eternal safety in the fortress of His name? He don't ask perfection—He *gives* it! He don't ask you to be saved already—He *saves* you! Don't you hear his voice a-calling you? Don't you know you got to answer? Don't you know you got to come? Don't you feel the pushing and the pulling of His holy spirit? Don't it make you restless? Oh, humble your hearts and come forward to receive His gift of love!"

Then I don't know what come over me. It was like I *did* feel a pulling and a pushing. They begun to sing once more, but I was too excited and riled up to join in. I felt like something— oh, something great and terrible!—was just about to happen to me. And I was ascared of it happening, yet I wanted it to, too. One part of me was saying, *Go on! You got to go!* when I seen the others streaming up the aisle and kneeling down—young folks and old, men and women . . . One woman I seen had a baby over her shoulder must have woken up with all the noise; I could see its face all red and squalling, looking back at me . . . That terrible time with Milo come back to me, when he suffered so bad, and then seen God; I thought I couldn't bear to suffer like he done, yet if Jesus taken me to His bosom in the end, I'd never need to feel no more fear. All around me, folks was hollering, "Take me, Lord!" and, "Glory be!" making so much racket I couldn't hear the preacher no more. They was many more jerking back and forth like that first feller done, or shouting or so—was a reglar Tower of Babel going on there. Then folks begun to sing, "Just as I am without one plea," and that was when I known I had to go. I stood up, all ready to head for the altar and give myself up to Jesus, when I found I couldn't move, because Milo had hold of my arm.

"No!" he says. "No!"

I turned round and looked at him, but it was like I didn't even see him. I don't know what it was got into me, because it seemed to me like Milo wasn't Milo no more—'twas the Devil sitting in his place, grabbing onto me, and if I didn't get loose, I'd be forever lost—God would give up on me and throw me to the Fool Killer like you'd throw a scrap to a hound dog. I give one big heave and snatched right out of my jacket, leaving the sleeve in Milo's hand. Then I hightailed it round the seats to where folks was kneeling down before the platform, and the preacher was on his knees hisself, praying for them.

19

When I try and recall what all happened at the camp meeting that night after I went up and got saved, I can see better how 'twas that Milo could of forgot all that happened to him before he was wounded. To my knowledge I wasn't hit on the head, but just the same I can't recollect nothing of it but bits and pieces, and none of them clear.

I can remember kneeling down with the rest of them up front, hollering and sobbing and praying like I was taking the worst licking of my life, yet at the same time feeling—I don't know, just grand! I've heared folks talk about the light within, and 'twas just so: I felt like something had touched fire to a candlewick inside me, and I could feel the hot wax from it running down, burning me and making me easy both at the same time. Finally, after I'd been carrying on and having that feeling for a while, I got weak as a kitten, like I had no more bones, and terrible drowsy, too. Somehow I known that Brother Arkwright was kneeling there beside me, though I couldn't recall just when he come, and I must of just leaned over against him and went to sleep. Anyways, I never known another thing until I woken up.

Then I didn't know where in the world I was. I was wrapped in a blanket with the knapsack under my head; what I was laying on was hard and they was something behind me was warm. Through the branches of the trees over me the sky was just gray dawn; when I turned my head sidewise I seen slats and I figured by the look of them I was in a wagon bed; what was warm beside me moved when I did and begun licking my face, which was Shep, Arkwrights' dog. Little by little, things from the night before come back to me, and I begun feeling round inside myself to find out how it was to be saved, like when you had a fall and move kind of cautious to find out is any bones broke. After a time I come to the conclusion I felt pretty much the same as ever, which was purely disappointing, because it looked to me like I wasn't born again after all. Then I thought: *Milo!* and I jumped up so quick I stepped on Shep's toe so he yelped; then I had to squat down and pet him and tell him I was sorry so's he wouldn't start in to bark.

'Twas one of Milo's blankets I'd been wrapped in, I seen, and his knapsack under my head, but I didn't know was it him put me there or Brother Arkwright, or who—yet if 'twas Milo, where could he be? . . . And then I remembered how when he'd asked me, I'd promised I wasn't interested in getting saved, only in singing hymns and seeing how folks carried on; how he tried to stop me from going up in front, but I snatched away, and I reckoned he must be plumb disgusted with me.

I better find him right away and tell him how it was and that I'm sorry and all, thinks I. Yet it seemed like it wouldn't be right to apologize for getting saved, neither—like as if that would be a slight on the Lord. *Well, I can just explain it to him,* I says to myself, and jumped down from the wagon bed. *When I tell him how it felt, Milo'll understand* . . . I started to go off, but Shep give a little whine, and I seen he was standing on the tail gate with his ears cocked and his tail wagging, trying to make up his mind to jump. So I lifted him down and he tagged after me.

The first notion come to me about where to look for Milo was how he never wanted to come to the meeting in the first place, how if it hadn't been for me begging he would of gone on round. So I figured he'd find a place to camp away from folks, yet not too far, so's in the morning he could come back to get me. And I knowed it would be somewheres pretty close to the water—in the trees, if he could find a private spot; if not, by a haystack or some shelter like in the fields. So I set off for the place where I done the dishes the night before, planning to scout up and down the stream.

All the folks in the camp was asleep—or, the way that preacher had it, the ones was saved, anyways . . . For all I'd of knowed, it could of been every man jack of them was, by the end of that meeting. Anyways, they was no one moving, neither in the tents nor them laying wrapped in blankets in wagon beds or on the ground. Shep started smelling the face of a feller snoring under a tree, so I picked him up and carried him till we come to the stream. The birds was striking up when we come by the water, and behind me I heared a rooster crow, though it wasn't yet what you'd call day.

I set Shep down and started off upstream, keeping a sharp eye on both banks for any sign of Milo. I walked along to the end of the trees; there I come to a long flat meadow, and just then the sun come up over the edge of the world so I seen the spiderwebs all shaking and sparkling with dew, and a long white rag of mist laying in a holler. Behind me I heared the sound of that horn was blowed the night before, and I thought I'd come a fair piece because it sounded far away. At t'other end of the field I seen what looked like a old haystack. *I bet that's where he is,* I thought, and struck off towards it, though it meant leaving the stream.

Shep went bounding out ahead of me through the tall grass, leaving a green trail in the dew, starting up a bobwhite once and chasing after it a piece. He come to the haystack ahead of me and begun to set up a yapping when he got there, like when he seen us the first time. *That's it, all right,* I says to myself. *Milo must be there.* I expected I'd see him getting up any minute, and I begun to try and think what I was going to say. It come back to me how relieved I felt when Milo told me them things he believed about sin—how they wasn't as much to it as preachers wanted you to think—and that made me feel more sheepish than ever about how I'd acted the night before. I didn't know how I'd explain it to him; I reckoned I'd just have to tell him how I'd felt, and maybe he could clear it up for me.

But as I come closer to the haystack, I begun to feel terrible disappointed, for nobody got up from beside it, and the way little Shep was raising Old Ned, no person could of gone on sleeping if he'd tried. *He ain't there,* I thought, and I begun to wonder where I'd look next. I could go back to the stream and foller it back t'other way, and that was what I'd have to do, yet it didn't seem likely he'd go downstream, because that was back towards where we come from, and Milo, he always liked to keep moving ahead.

"Here, Shep!" I hollers. "You, Shep! Come back here!"

When he heared my voice he turned his head toward me and stopped barking a minute; then he started in again. First I felt mad with him for being such a pesky critter, and like to turned round and left him there; then I begun to feel curious what in Tophet he *was* carrying on so over if Milo or no one wasn't there. So I kept on towards him until I got pretty near, which was when I seen he was standing by something dark on the ground which he put his nose down and smelled ever now and then before he started in to bark some more. Some way my heart begun to pound, and I broke into a run—until I was near enough to see 'tweren't but a piece of cloth or a old coat or so laying there.

90

"What ails you?" I says to Shep. "If you ain't the feeble-mindedest dog!"

But he kept right on barking until I come up and picked the thing up from the ground. Then he stopped and stood there with his tongue hanging out and his tail wagging.

Why, 'twas tother one of our blankets!

And it was all marked up with some kind of dark stain—some places just on the nap; others, soaked right through.

It wasn't water and it wasn't coffee and it was kind of sticky like—and I begun to shake all over because the onliest thing I could think of it *could* be was blood.

20

I bundled that blanket under my arm, turned round, and begun to run. My heart was going like a sledge hammer and my breathing hurt me, yet I kept running anyways, back over the green track Shep and me had made in the wet grass. Shep frolicked round me in circles like we was playing a game; when we come to the edge of the trees near the stream bank I tripped over him and fell; then I just lay on the ground panting with Shep standing by me, licking my ear. When my breathing got slower, I set up, and something made me look at my hands. Where I'd been clutching onto the blanket, the right one was rusty red.

Milo! I thought. *Milo!* And that was all the further I could go.

Then for some reason—I never did know why—I taken the blanket, rolled it up tight, and, standing on my tippy toes, I wedged it in the crotch of a limb of a little pin oak. After that I jumped the creek and headed back downstream towards the camp.

As I come near, I could hear voices the way you hear water running before you come in sight of it, and they was something fast and excited about them, the way you can tell when it's a rapids, not just a ordinary river or stream. Shep left me and run on ahead—or else it was me slowed down. And when I come in sight of the clearing, I seen there was surely something besides preaching happening there.

Folks was all gathered together in bunches in the clearing, standing amongst the logs, women together and men together, mostly. I seen a couple of fellers with rifles under their arm. *What is it, oh, what is it?* I thought, but something told me to go slow; to come up easy; not to ask no questions, just see what I could hear.

I circled round the clearing, looking for a good place to sidle up to some folks so's they wouldn't notice how I come there. I seen Brother Arkwright in a circle of men, talking and waving his arms. I seen his ma, too, in another part of the clearing, holding Shep, with him barking away. But I didn't want to go near neither of them, so, thinking it was a good time to get the blanket and knapsack from their wagon, I skinned round to their camp and taken them. Just as I was fixing the blanket over my shoulder with a piece of string, a voice behind me says:

"Hey, you, what you at?"

I whirled round, but 'tweren't nothing but a fat old red-headed boy, no biggern me.

"I'm getting my traps," I says, "if it's any business of yours."

"Oh no!" he says. "I reckon it ain't no business of mine, see-ing as how no little shrimp like you never murdered nobody, even if I never did clap eyes on you before and I know most everbody else at this here meeting."

Another time I would of taken off the knapsack and blanket again and fit him—I already said he weren't no biggern me except for being fat—but right then I didn't even think of it.

"What you talking of murdering for?" I says.

"What am I *talking* of it for?" says he. "What ails you? Ain't nobody talking of nothing else! Wait a minute—you mean you ain't *heared?*"

"Heared what?" says I.

"Are you deaf and dumb, or what?"

My hands was shaking, so I put them in my pockets, but my voice come out pretty good. "Listen," I says, "I—I woken up early and sneaked off fishing. I didn't—I never even heared the horn blow. I—I ain't anxious to meet up with my pa, neither. Most likely he'll tan my hide."

Something just told me to lie like that, and it come pretty easy, only I hoped he wouldn't ask me which one was my pa. But he says:

"Where's your fish?"

"Didn't catch none. Go on and tell it—what's going on?"

He looked purely pleased. "The preacher got kilt," he says. "Reverend Spotts."

"The preacher?" I says, and let out a great sigh. "Kilt? The one preached last night?"

"Say, don't you know nothing?" says he. He was reglar spoiling for a fight, but I couldn't oblige him just then.

"My folks just got here last evening," says I. "How did he get kilt?"

"Chopped with his own ax!" he says. "Just about left in pieces! They found him in his tent a-swimming in his own blood! That was at breakfast time when he didn't come round to the Widder Perriman's tent to eat like he usually done. She had the high-sterics. You could of heared her in the next county. Lucky thing my ma brought her smelling salts on account of having the sick headaches!"

"You—you seen him?"

He looked disgusted. "Naw," he says. "They won't let nobody near. But I aim to sneak round the back of the tent when things is more quieted down. You want to come, too?"

I says, "No."

"What's the matter—a-scared of blood? Anybody a-scared of blood ain't no better'n a girl!"

"I ain't a-scared," I says. "Who they think done it?" Inside my pocket, I could feel the stickiness on my hand.

"They don't *think*," he says. "They *know!*"

"Well, who?"

" 'Twas Whiskey Pete."

"Who's that?"

"Oh my, if you was any more ignorant they'd plant you for a potato! Don't you know *nothing?* Whiskey Pete sells whiskey."

"Right here? At camp meeting?" says I.

He rolls up his eyes. "Lord give me patience!" he says. "You must be *backward,* I reckon. Whiskey Pete goes to ever camp meeting in this county."

"You mean he comes right up and sells whiskey to folks at meeting?"

"Oh my, yes, puddenhead, he climbs right up on the platform by the preacher and gives out a bottle to everone saved."

"Looky here," I says, taking a step towards him, "if you're all that itchy for a fight, I'll give it to you, you big tub of lard! Ain't no crime never to of been to a camp meeting, and it ain't

93

no sin not to hail from hereabouts neither. But if it's trouble you're looking for, just say the word and I'll give it to you—right in that big soft belly of yourn!"

Soon as I come forward, he backed up. "Ain't *you* techy!" he says, and I knowed he weren't nothing but a cowardy-custard after all.

"All right," I says. "Just mind your manners if you don't want no bloody nose. Why do they think it was this here Whiskey Pete done—done it?"

"Why because," he says, "the Reverend Spotts was fixing to have the Knights of the Soul Reborn ride him on a rail—and besides, they already found his still and busted it." I give him a look, and he went on real quick. "I reckon you wouldn't know who the Knights was, neither. Well, they're like a sheriff's posse, see, of fellers been saved and goes around rooting up sin. Why, they caught Mattie Simmons kissing in the bushes and they taken her to her pa and said if he didn't lick her, they would, and they ducked the feller kissing her in the creek . . . Surely wouldn't of seemed worth it to me, even if Mattie didn't have the cast in one eye."

"Stick to the point," says I. "What about Whiskey Pete?"

"Well, what else you want to know? Like I said, Pete comes round to all the meetings, but of course he don't come up near like peddlers that's just selling combs or jackknives or candy or lemonade or anything ain't lures of the Devil. He hides his wagon out in the woods somewheres, where it's hard to find but not too hard, so folks can sneak out and buy a bottle off him. But this here particular meeting is hard by where Pete lives. So when Reverend Spotts got the Knights to going—that was a new idea he got up this year—they combed the countryside and busted up the still. But everybody known it was Reverend Spotts behind it all. So now the Knights has gone off to Pete's place to find him and bring him back, and most likely string him up."

Just then, a woman's voice called out from the clearing:

"St. Elmo! Come here! You, St. Elmo! I mean *you!*"

"That's my ma," the boy says. "I got to go. Say, you want to creep round and see the corpse with me later when I can get away?"

"Maybe," I says. "I'll see."

"I'll look for you," he says, and with that went off, with that two-sided look fat folks got when they run.

Now folks in the clearing was commencing to move about, like they might be fixing to come back to their camps, but I

94

didn't want to meet up with none of them or have to talk to them. So I started back through the trees. Behind me, a man called out:

"Where you going, son?"

I almost cut and run, but I stopped myself and says, "In the bushes."

"Well, don't stray too far."

Then I headed for the creek again, but back downstream where it come out of the grove near the spot Shep barked at us the night before. When I was out of the trees it made me feel too out in the open some way; I run for a clump of willows down the bank like something was at my heels. They grown slantwise over the water with their long green branches hanging down; I crept under them, and they covered me like a house.

21

I set down, wrapped my arms round my knees, and put my head down on them. Seemed like I couldn't understand nothing had happened that morning, and I just set still, hid amongst the branches of the willow tree, not thinking anything at all. First I set with my eyes shut; then I lifted up my head and opened them. Staring at the water going by, I seen fish in it—little ones, but big enough to eat. So I untied the blanket and unstrapped the knapsack; I taken a hook and line out of my pocket and baited with a bit of side meat; I set there fishing— I don't know how long. First my head was just empty. Then thoughts and ideas and wonderings begun to gather there, like storm clouds on a clear day.

Milo's dead, was the first thing come to me. It didn't seem sad or nothing. Just *He's dead*, like one of them dreams you have when you're dead yourself and it don't seem no different from being alive. There I was, setting fishing with the sun shining and the breeze stirring the willow branches like curtains at a window, so how could he be dead?

I felt a bite on the line, pulled it in, and taken the fish off the hook. When I laid it down on the grass, I seen I already had two others laying there. I thought: *When did I catch them?* but I couldn't remember doing it or taking them off the hook at all. I baited the hook and thrown it back in, though the three was moren a plenty for me.

Then I thought: *Why, no! 'Tweren't Milo was kilt. 'Twas the preacher.* And that was the first I knowed of how I must of taken it for granted Milo was dead all the time. From the time I found the blanket. And then I met the boy that told me it was the preacher. 'Twasn't Milo. 'Twas the preacher. Or, 'twasn't Milo, so far as I *knowed*.

And yet it seemed like Milo was dead to me. It didn't seem real, but it seemed true.

The boy said, *They know who kilt the preacher. They don't think it, they know it*. But why in the world would Whiskey Pete want to kill Milo?

Listen, I says to myself, *you don't even know Milo's dead!*

But I couldn't keep my mind from going right along the same way.

Maybe Milo come along and catched Whiskey Pete when he was amurdering the preacher, so he went for Milo, too . . .

Then how did the blanket get off by the haystack?

Well, supposen Milo was carrying the blanket on his way to make camp when he passed the preacher's tent, seen Whiskey Pete after the preacher and tried to stop him. Then Whiskey Pete turned on him, too, but Milo managed to get away. He was wounded, but he made it to the haystack . . . But then why would he go off again and leave the blanket?

Whiskey Pete, Whiskey Pete. Most likely it was something in the name, but ever time I thought of him, all I could see was a kind of jolly dirty old feller like Jim which you couldn't imagine doing no harm. I knowed that if he'd killed the preacher, I must of been wrong, only I couldn't make it seem to myself like he'd of killed Milo too.

Look, I says to myself, *whoever told you Milo's dead?*

And inside my head, something else answers back, *The blood told me. That's who.*

All of a sudden I says out loud, "Oh, please, God, don't let Milo be dead!" and I hollered right out and hit my fists on the ground because everthing seemed so terrible and I didn't know what to do. And who was I going to ask when Milo wasn't there?

I'll go back, I thought. *I'll find Brother Arkwright and tell him about the blanket*. And I got up and was all ready to run back to the grove when I froze like a rabbit and set down again, real slow.

I forgot, I thought. *Oh Lordy, how could I of forgot?* I'd forgot Milo's enemies.

He never did want to go in that grove. He never did want to stay for the meeting. He only done it because he seen I wanted to so bad. But wouldn't he of *told* me if he was walking into a ambush or trap and knowed it? I *said* to him it weren't all that important to me! I *told* him it didn't make no difference —I'd just as soon go round! Why, 'twas me seen that church steeple, made us cut off the road, and come that way at all! That was because I knowed about strange cities being the places of his enemies. And besides, he said he always knowed when they was near. If that was so, why wouldn't he know this time?

Then I remembered the day he had the spell, how he'd said to me they was near and had been mistook. Because if they'da been laying for him anywheres that time, they could of had him for sure, with him sick, and me, the only one to fight for him, nothing but a boy. If he was mistook about them that time, then he could of been mistook this time, too, only tother way round. Maybe they *was* near but he never felt it at all . . . Or maybe he was just beginning to feel it when I begun to pester him to see what the doings was and put it out of his mind.

I got to have help, I thought. *I got to tell somebody.* And Brother Arkwright come to my mind again. I'd tell about the blanket, and he'd get them Knights together. But I wouldn't tell about Milo's enemies, because . . .

Wait a minute, I says to myself. *Hold on. Go slow.* Because another something come to me. Like Milo's voice—or the memory of it, anyways—speaking to me.

All men was his brothers, Milo used to say. And I asked him, *If all men is your brothers, how come some is your enemies? Cain and Abel was brothers, wasn't they?* says he. And Brother Arkwright, when he come up and greeted us, what did he say? "We're all brethren and sistern here."

Take it easy, I says to myself again. *Hold your horses.*

Whiskey Pete weren't one of them brethren, that was one thing sure. Maybe 'twas him hurted Milo and maybe not. But supposen 'twasn't him, and supposen Milo weren't dead after all. Supposen he was wounded and holed up somewheres, but whoever done it had left him for dead, thinking he'd finished the job. Then I'd go back there and set them all to searching for him. They wasn't a one of them I could be sure wasn't his enemies. I could go right up to the very one done it and lead him to Milo. I could of been his brother, Milo always said, but if I was to do that, I'd be no bettern a Cain.

No. I wasn't going to do it. If 'twas me lost, what would Milo of done? Found me and cared for me—not put no enemies on my trail. *I ain't but a boy,* I thought, *but this is one time I got to act like a man, even if I don't know how. I'll try to think what Milo would of done, and whatever it is, that will be the best way. One thing's sure, I got to do it alone. I'll make me a camp away from the grove somewheres, and I'll comb this here countryside until I find him, dead or alive!*

And if I wasn't to find him—if I didn't find him—I didn't know what I'd do.

22

So the first thing I done was build me a fire and clean my fish and eat them, because I known I'd never do nothing right on a empty stomach. Next I taken my knapsack and blanket, and, circling wide around the fields, I come back to the haystack where Shep and me found the blanket, and hid my things in the hay. It might just be he'd come back there, I thought. Then I begun to hunt, beginning with the banks of the stream, because I remembered from different tales Milo told me of the war—after he got out the hospital and went back, that is—how the first thing wounded fellers cry for is water. I searched for him in a different part ever day, sometimes going so far 'twas almost nightfall when I got back to the haystack. But I'd never camp nowheres else, because it never stopped seeming to me like some time I'd get back to it and find him there.

I kept wide of the meeting ground so long as they was folks still there—I never sneaked close enough to hear what was going on for fear somebody'd foller me; I didn't even find out did they catch Whiskey Pete or hang him or what, but, after a couple of days, I seen the wagons moving out of the grove; they was no more smoke from the fires, and after that I felt both lonesome and relieved; I went back to the camp grounds when

I was sure they was all gone and searched around there, but all I found was a broke Jew's harp, a comb, and a book called *The Missionary's Friend*. Nothing that was anything of Milo's at all.

Little by little, after I'd been searching for him all day ever day, it got so I couldn't hope no more, because I never found a trace of him nowheres. More and more it seemed like I hadn't no thoughts left to think that wasn't mournful and gloomy and made me sick at heart.

I begun to believe he must of been kilt like the preacher, only drug off Lord knows where so's a person couldn't even put a stone up for his grave—left all bloody and broke for the buzzards to pick his bones. Seemed like I could see a picture of him sometimes, laying in a lonesome spot, with his mouth open and his beard all dark with gore. Whenever that come to me, I got so I'd just pitch down on the ground and bawl for grief, wherever I was. *Oh, Milo, Milo!* I'd think. *I don't want it to be so!*

You'd think that would of make me feel worse than anything, yet there was something come to me later made me feel even more low.

No! I'd answer it. *That ain't true! Milo never would of done such a thing, even if I did make him mad! We was brothers, almost, like he always said! He'd never go off and leave me that way!*

But it would go on plaguing me, like the Devil tempting a person to sin.

Why wouldn't he? it'd say. *He told you he never wanted to go to that meeting, but you made him. You promised him you never cared nothing about getting saved, but you snatched away from him when he tried to stop you, and there you was on your knees, crying and repenting like some fool girl, first dash out the box.*

Listen, I'd tell it, *if I'd just have a chance to explain it to him, Milo'd understand. Milo could understand anything; he'd never hold it against me that way!*

But it wouldn't leave me be. *Anyways,* it'd say, *what's a growed man want with a boy tagging after his heels like a hound dog, only not so much use all day?*

I never tagged! I'd tell it. *Even when I had the blister I kept up good's a man!*

. . . Chattering at him, asking questions all the while, never giving him no peace.

He liked to talk to me! He said so over and over. Milo did! He said he admired to have me for his comrade! He said we was two good soldiers, keeping each other company on the road!

Oh yes, he was a mighty polite man! He wouldn't of hurt the feelings of a fly. You could of drove him right to the end of his patience without him ever letting on.

"I never, I never!" I'd shout right out loud. "I kept quiet whenever I seen he was thinking, and if he'd of asked me, I'd of laid down for him and died!"

And then I'd wish that instead of Milo had just up and taken French leave of me that way—if that was what he done— I *had* laid down and died, or even, ruther than it was so (oh, I knowed I'd go to hell for thinking it, all right!), but I'd ruther he *was* kilt—yes I would!—and laying dead somewheres than that he'd lit out and left me without even saying no goodbye. He could of told me if he couldn't stand to have me round no more! He ought to of knowed I'd stand up to it like a man!

I ate up the side meat was left in the knapsack, and fish I catched, and went on combing the woods and fields round about, even when it seemed to me it wasn't much use no more. After the camp meeting folks was gone, I never seen a human soul, but I made friends with a old collie dog come sniffing round the haystack after me one day, and then I had him to talk to when he'd come back again from time to time. I guess it wasn't more than a few days, but it seemed to me like a hundred years I stayed there—until the side meat give out and the fish wouldn't bite and I got so hungry I would of eat a old shoe. So I give up, finally. I recollect how it was a bright sunny day with the fields all green and shining. I looked up in the blue sky and I says, "I hate you, God!" as ugly as I knowed how, which made me feel better some way, and anyhow kept me from busting out crying.

Then I put on the blanket and knapsack and went back towards the road Milo and me was going along that last day when we seen we was coming to a town. My idea was this time I'd keep on until I got to it, and when I did, I'd steal something— the first thing to eat I seen handy, like maybe a hot apple pie— and get caught and put in jail so's I could just give over troubling, and anyways not be hungry no more.

And if they asked me my name, I'd never tell them, or I'd say, Joe Smith, or so, and make up some other things to say— and then how'd they know to send me back to him and the Old Crab, even if they was to try?

And I thought how if I ever seen Milo again, I'd tell him how I might of got saved that once, but I was good and backslidden now.

THE GALTS
23

When I come to the road, the dust of it felt warm on my feet. I walked along pretty brisk for a ways until all of a sudden I kicked up something which didn't feel like a stone or a button or a piece of glass or something you'd expect to find. So I stooped down to look, and there was a quarter of a dollar laying before my eyes. I picked it up, spit on it, shined it on my sleeve, but it weren't no mistake. Somebody had dropped it and there it stayed, waiting for me, saving me from committing a crime and going to jail—for a while, anyways. I looked up at the sky and thought of dropping on my knees to apologize some way, but I felt too foolish right out there in the road, and then it come to me that probly I was pretty small potatoes for God to of noticed one way or t'other anyhow. So I put it in my pocket and started off again at a right smart pace.

First I seen the steeple again and then the whole town showed through the trees. 'Twasn't but a little place, and put me in mind of a big bed with the church at one end for the headboard and the store at t'other for the foot. By the sun, it was about noon then, and they wasn't a human being in sight, only a couple of dogs sleeping or scratching fleas in the sun, and down by the store a wagon with a mule, switching his tail and flicking his ears at flies. I reckoned everone was in their house eating dinner; seemed like my nose worked extra good when I was hungry, so I could smell ever dish on ever table as I went by— roast pork and applesauce and corn bread and lemon pie and baked sweet potatoes. I walked past em all with my mouth watering, and even the dogs was too lazy to pay me any mind, so I felt like a ghost nobody could see.

At the other end, when I come to the store, I stopped a minute; then I hitched up my pants and went in the door. They was a big maple in front made it shady and dark in there; when I first come in, I couldn't see nothing after coming out of the sun. But a voice says, "Howdo," and I begun to make out a woman setting in a rocker towards the back.

"Howdy," says I, and she got up and set her work on the case.

"What can I do for you?" she asks.

"Cheese," I says, because I seen it right in front of me behind the glass, and my mouth begun to water, so's I could hardly talk. "I'd like some cheese, please, mam."

"Yes, sir," she says, opening the back of the case. "How much you want?"

"I got a quarter," I says, but then I thinks: *I got to get something else besides.* "And can I have some crackers, too?"

She had the cheese half out when she put it back, straightened up, and looked at me.

"I seen you some place before," she says. "Some place."

She was just a ordinary-looking woman with a plain-looking face and hair color hair, not old enough to be nobody's granny, but old enough to be somebody's ma, clean and neat in a blue dress, with nothing about her to notice at all—except she begun to look at me odd, and it made me wonder should I turn tail and run right then and there, though I didn't yet know any reason why.

"Wait a minute!" she says, squinting up her eyes. "It'll come to me! Yes, I seen you out to the meeting. But it can't be your folks lives round here."

"No'm," I says, and taken a step back.

"You visiting here in town?"

"No'm," says I, and taken another step towards the door.

"Is your folks waiting outside for you?" she says. "Ask them to come in and rest thesselves. It's a right hot day to be on the road."

"I—I ain't—no, thank you, mam. I'll just go along now."

"Why, you never got your cheese!"

"That's all right," I says. "I don't mind."

I had my hand on the doorframe and was all ready to turn round and run when she says, "Hold on!" and it stopped me—maybe because if I had started to run, I wouldn't of knowed which way to go. "Just tell me this," she says. "Are you traveling by yourself? Are you alone?"

My voice stuck in my throat so I couldn't answer it at all, only stare at her. And while I was looking in her face, something happened to it which I couldn't exactly explain. It changed —only I don't know what about it *did* change, for she didn't smile or frown or nothing—no, 'twas something about the eyes.

102

"Nobody's trying to keep you," she says, like she known what I was thinking—all the time looking at me that queer way. "You're free to go any time, but they's something I'd like to ask you. My husband and me are looking for a boy to help out here, and I wondered if you might like the job. Yes," she says, and then she looks right out over my head with her eyes so bright and strange, "we certainly have been looking for a boy!"

I reckon I looked like a statue, just standing staring at her. I didn't say nothing, just looked, and while I was looking, I seen her eyes change back to plain.

"Mind," she says, "I can't undertake to hire you without Mr. Galt sees you and has the final say. And I wouldn't be surprised if he was to want to try you out a while first, same as you'd want a few days to see if you'd care to stay. But if you think you might consider it, you could come out back and have a bite of dinner now and wait till Mr. Galt comes home."

But I was still dumfounded. It seemed so queer. What'd she want of me? Wasn't they no other boys in that town? I kind of had the feeling—I don't know why—that she'd never thought of hiring no boy until she clapped eyes on me, nor her husband neither—yet if they hadn't, what was she up to anyways? Only she was such a ordinary woman, like I said, not mean looking, or nosy looking, or even finicky looking, but just plain . . . Except for that odd way her eyes changed when she'd stopped looking plain. They'd been something like I knowed her about the way she looked then, only I was pretty sure I'd never seen her before. No, it was more like she looked like somebody else I'd knowed, yet I couldn't place who . . . And then, all at once I thought that who she'd looked like then was Milo. I don't know why, because there wasn't nothing like him about her. And I begun to bawl.

I just stood there with my eyes screwed shut and the tears running down my face, so ashamed I thought I should die. All I could think of was that if she come near me or any way touched me, I'd have to cut and run. I didn't want to run—I didn't know where to run to—but I felt it coming sure as fate: she'd touch me and I'd have to run, want to or not—just thinking about it made me bawl more, dry kind of sobs that didn't make no noise, like being sick to my stomach, and my eyes squeezed shut, and waiting for her to touch me all the while. Yet it didn't happen and didn't happen; finally, still bawling, I had to open my eyes. I seen then she had her back turned to me and was sticking her crochet hook in her work and rolling it up in a towel.

"You're hungry," she says. "Come along now and wash your face and hands and I'll fix you a plate of something. Then you can make up your mind." And she passed out the door at the back of the store without giving so much as a look to see if I was coming after her.

I was, all right, and not thinking no more of it than a friendly pup following a tramp. Behind her back I wiped the tears off on my sleeve, and sniffled some until I reckoned I didn't look so bad. We went down a kind of long dark hall and come out in a kitchen where the sun was shining in the window and door; she shown me the sink and give me a towel and soap; while I washed, she taken a cold ham out the oven, and a mess of beans from the larder; she cut me a square of gingerbread from a pan; went outside and come back in a minute with a big crock of milk all dewed over with cold sweat, and a little one of butter.

"There," she says. "Eat slow, but eat hearty."

I done my best not to hog it, but that food just seemed to melt away; she filled my plate again without even asking did I want some more. While I was polishing off the second lot, she taken the milk and butter crocks back outside; she didn't come back right away, and when I was done, I felt my eyes drooping and my head so heavy that I just laid it down on the table for a minute; the last things I can remember was some flies buzzing round the ceiling; a cow bell somewheres not far away, the chickens clucking out back, and somebody whistling for a dog down towards the other end of town. After that, I was asleep so deep that she must of picked me up, lugged me in the downstairs bedroom, and covered me with a quilt without I fluttered an eyelid; next thing I knowed she was shaking me; I seen it was night by the lamp lighted on the dresser; she was pulling off my shirt and pants and putting me in a nightshirt. Then I was asleep again; the next thing it was morning with the birds singing and the sun shining outside; I was tangled up in that nightshirt like it was a feed sack, and I was in the bed between the sheets where she must of got me without I known it at all.

24

When I got myself straightened round in that nightshirt so's my hands was out the sleeves anyways, I just lain there in that bed, feeling of it. I was the way you are when you could wake up or go to sleep again either one just as easy, and it was like I was laying on a cloud, I hadn't slept in a bed for so long. I surely did have me a sleep that time!

But I'd had my fill of it, I reckon, for I kept waking up a little piece at a time, and presently had to start in to thinking. Of where I'd been, where I was, and what was I going to do next. I couldn't lay there forever. I was going to have to get up shortly, put my clothes on, and find somebody. Find that woman. And talk to her. Oh, I could hear them questions coming like a engine down the tracks! Who's your folks, where you come from, and so on.

My clothes was laying on a chair. I seen through the window 'twasn't no drop from there to the ground. All I'd need to do would be step over the sill and I could be gone again. Find a depot, ride the cars, travel West. Outside, I heard the birds singing. Robins, I could make out, and somewheres nearby, a phoebe. "Phoebe!" it says. "Phoebe!" And then it says, "Milo!" instead, and I stuck my head under the pillow and begun to bawl. I didn't want to go nowheres by myself no more. I felt like a reglar baby and ready to admit it. I says, "I'm scared!" just to of said it into the mattress there, knowing nobody could hear. My head was full of remembering—how 'twould be walking down a road with Milo on a beautiful bright day like today, and other things I didn't want to think about at all. Then I begun to feel kind of smothered, and pulled my head out and quit bawling.

I can stay, thinks I. *Ain't no reason for not staying, if I play my cards right. Anyways, she said to me 'twould only be to try it out, to begin with. All I got to do is think up a good water-tight lie and tell it with a straight face. I'll look her right in the eye. Only first I got to think what it's to be. And I known* it was pretty late—if I didn't get it ready pretty quick, she'd be coming in to see if I'd died, or lit out, and I'd be caught short.

I'll tell her I'm a orphan, I thought, *but not that my folks died long ago, like I done with Miz Fanshawe, because then I'll just have to make up extra about where I been since. No. I'll tell her my folks died not long ago. Of the typhoid fever, which is true.* Struck me then how the best lies is the ones which has most truth in them. *And what next? What would a feller do when his folks died? Well, move in with kin. So why ain't I with kin?*

Then it all come to my mind, kind of beautiful and easy, like I was reading a tale. I'd tell it like this: I was on my way to stay with my cousins lived in—Passerel, but when I got there, I found the house all shut up. So I went next door and asked the folks lived there, "Where's—where's Aunt Myra and Uncle Jim?" And the woman says, "Sakes alive, boy, didn't you know they sold their house and headed West?" So I told how my folks had died and I had wrote ahead to say I was coming, but didn't wait for a answer, just come after my letter, because I knowed Aunt Myra and Uncle Jim would admire to have me on account of Aunt Myra being my mother's sister. My mother's favorite sister. So then the woman says she didn't know just where it was they was going, but they wasn't gone but a day or so, and if I hurried along, I might catch up with them. Just go through the woods and take the turnpike, she says. So I did, but I never seen nor heard of them, though I asked everwheres I passed through, and I couldn't see they was no more use in trying to find them now . . . There, wouldn't that do?

After a minute, I seen it wouldn't, because supposen she decided to write back to Passerel and come to find they wasn't never no such folks there?

"Oh, durn it all!" I says, and give the pillow a thump and jumped out of bed. If she done that, by the time she gotten a letter back, I'd—I'd run away again. And I was tired of thinking, and I wanted some breakfast, anyways. *Listen,* I wished I dast say to her, *you wouldn't ask me no such questions if I was a growed man! Ain't it a free country?* I wished I'd have the nerve to say. Then I put on my clothes and opened the door. They was a dark hallway outside, and at one end of it a voice singing a tune, which sounded like it might be hers. So I went that way.

I come out in the kitchen, all bright and full of sun, with her washing up crockery at the sink and singing. I cleared my throat so's not to give her a start, and she turned.

"Good morning," she says. "You're quite a sleeper for a boy your age."

"Yes, mam," I says. "Good morning."

"My sink's full," she says, "so I reckon it won't kill you to eat dirty this once. Set down."

I set at the table; she dried her hands and handed me a apple from a bowl of them on the winder sill; then she dished up some porridge was standing on the stove, poured me coffee with lots of cream and sweetening, just the way I like it best. While I ate, she went back to dishwashing and singing, and I was glad not to have to talk. But I was done, finally, and brought my dishes over to her. She put them in the soapy water, dried her hands again, taken me by the shoulder, and pushed me over towards the table—not hard, though. "Set down again," she says. "I reckon you and me has to have a little talk, haven't we?"

I set down on one side, she set down on the other, put her elbows on the table, and folded her hands. "You know," she says, "you never got a chance to even tell me your name."

"No, mam," I says, kind of tightening up and getting ready. "It's George Mellish, mam."

"Well, mine is Louisa Galt," says she, "and my husband is Mr. Samuel Galt. They's just the two of us lives in the house here and runs the store. So you see, we can use a boy to help out, and for company, too, not having our own family."

I didn't say nothing, just waited for what was to come.

"When you know me better, George," she says, "you'll find out I ain't a person to pry. But they's some questions I'll have to ask you now—that is, if you think you'd like to stay. Would you, George?"

"I—yes, mam. I reckon I would."

"In that case, I guess Mr. Galt and me would like to know where you're from."

"I'm from—Farway," I says. "That's back East a piece."

"Farway," she says. "I never heard tell of that town." Neither had I, since I just that minute made it up, but, shucks, they's many towns nobody ever heard of. "And what about your folks, George? Where are they?"

"Dead," I says, clenching up my fists in my lap to get ready for the lie.

"Oh dear, I'm real sorry, George!" she says. "Have they been dead long?"

"No, mam," I says. "Not but a couple of months."

She put her hand out acrost the table like she meant to touch me, then took it back again. "That's hard," she says. "Ain't nothing to say but it's hard." And I felt downright ashamed. But I just clenched my fists more tight. "Didn't you have no relatives to take you in?"

Then all of a sudden I felt all betwixt and between, because I seen I didn't need to go on with the rest of what I made up at all—all I needed to say was no, and I'd be clear. Only I'd planned it t'other way, and it seemed like it might be safer not to change my plan. "No," I says, kind of choked sounding, "not there."

"Do you have some somewheres else?"

"Yes, mam. Leastways I thought I did."

"How was that, George?" she says. "What do you mean?"

So then I brought out my tale just like I'd planned it, and I thought it sounded pretty good. She listened like she believed ever word, and when I was through, she says, "But, George, they must be a way to find them! I don't know what, but we'll ask Mr. Galt, and he'll think of a idea! Must be folks back there known where your aunt and uncle was going besides just them folks you asked from next door. I don't know what they was thinking of, sending a homeless boy off on a wild goose chase like that and never even stopping to make inquiries or nothing!" And her face got pink like she was thinking of them folks which I'd made up out of whole cloth, and wished she could tell them a thing or two.

Then I felt awful sorry I'd lied to her. I didn't know what else I could of did, but one thing I was sure of now was I wanted to stay there and work for them pretty bad, and, right then, another lie come to me which looked like the only way out.

"Wait, mam," I says. "I ain't told you the whole tale. Later on, while I was traveling along, I met up with some folks on their way back from the West, and they was telling all about a awful Injun massacree. Oh, 'twas a regular hair-raiser, all about how the mother and the two little girls with long golden curls was scalped, and the house—I mean the wagon—was set fire to and burned to a cinder. And then they says, 'That poor Jelliman family!' and I says to them, 'Jelliman? Which Jelliman you mean?' and they says, 'James and Myra Jelliman, they was,' and then I knowed 'twas my kin they was talking of, and 'tweren't no use for me to look for them no more."

Then she looked at me. She just looked, and I knowed *she* knowed I'd told a lie.

Sure enough, she says, "George, that ain't true!"

"True?" I says. "Well, I only know what they told me, Miz Galt, mam."

"It ain't true nobody told you that," she says.

Then it was like you're stacking wood and you do it wrong and the whole thing falls down. I got up from the table. "I can't help it if you don't believe me!" I says.

She says, "Oh yes, you can!"

I couldn't stand it the way she was looking at me, and all of a sudden I yells at her, "You wouldn't ask a growed man no such questions! What right you got to ask me just because I'm nothing but a boy?"

Then her eyes changed, and they wasn't two blue drills going right through me finding out the lies no more. She even looked like she might be getting ready to laugh, which made me mad. "Set down, George," she says. "Set down and calm down. We can talk about this quiet. I got a right to ask you questions I wouldn't ask a man because you ain't a man. You ain't yet old enough to take care of yourself. You're most old enough, but not quite. And so long as a boy *is* a boy and not a man, it's the business of the growed folks around him to see he's took care of as best they can. Now listen to me. You could of skinned out the winder this morning and I'd never of seed you again. I don't know if you thought of it or not, but I did. That's why I'll let you walk out this door free as air, if that's what you want. I could hold you some, but not much, and not forever, if you didn't want to stay. But if you do want to, you got to answer some questions truthful, because they's some things I got to know. If you don't care to, just say, 'I don't want to stay,' and you can go. Is that agreeable to you?"

"Yes'm," I says, "I guess so," and I set down.

"Was it the truth that your folks is dead, George?"

"Yes, mam," says I.

"Have you got kin someplace you know of?"

"No, mam," says I.

"Honest and true, George?"

I looked her right in the eye. "Cross my heart and hope to die!"

"Then they's just one more thing. Is they anyone—anyone at all—who's grieving for you and worrying over you—even if they was cantankerous with you sometimes, or scolded you, or licked you? Just take a minute, George, and ask your own heart, because if you was to be hurting others, I wouldn't want no part in that."

109

"I swear I ain't. Miz Galt," I says. "They ain't a living soul gives a durn about me!"

"Why, that's all then!" she says, and got up quick. "There, that wasn't near as bad as having a tooth out, was it? Now come along and see Mr. Galt."

25

So I follered after her down that dark hallway back to the store. When we got there, 'twas full of folks, buying things, or looking round, waiting.

"My land, Mr. Galt, why didn't you call me?" she says.

"Figgered you was busy," he answers, going right on about his business, which right then was weighing something on a big brass scales.

"George, you set back here in the rocker till we take care of these folks," she says, and went down behind the counter with him.

I felt kind of extry and noticeable, so I pulled the chair halfways behind a barrel and leaned back in it; then 'twas as good as a hidey-hole, for 'twas darkish back there. That tree outside made the whole store dim and greeny all day long, even up by the windows; first off folks looked just black to me against the light, but then I begun to make out faces. 'Twas him I was staring at mostly—Mr. Galt, I mean.

He was bald, but his hair weren't gray, what he had left. Mrs. Galt, she talked right along while she waited on folks, asking how was this one or that one in a person's family, and things like that, but he just seemed to speak when spoke to, and then not much. He was a pretty big feller—a head tallern her, anyways, and she weren't what you'd call sawed off—but they got round each other behind the counter there neat as grand right and left and dosie-do. Pretty soon all the folks was took care of and cleared out so they wasn't none left but me and the Galts.

"All right, George," she says then. "Come on up, now, and meet Mr. Galt. Mr. Galt, here's George Mellish. He's decided he'd like to stay on and try out the job."

I come out and stepped up to him; we shook hands.

"Howdy, sir," I says, and he says:

"Howdo, George."

"I guess you menfolks got things to talk over," she says, "so I'll go back and get at my housework now."

"Well now, wait a minute," says he. "I don't know what we got to talk about you hadn't ought to hear. Twenty-five cents a week and keep agreeable to you, George?"

I hadn't given it a thought yet, but I says, "Yes, sir, I reckon so." I put my hand in my pocket and felt of that quarter of a dollar I found in the road. I never before in my life had moren a cent at a time—to keep, I mean. This way, in three weeks I'd have enough to change it all in for a cartwheel—how'd *that* be to reach right down in your pocket and feel?

"But I think we better bank some of that for you, George," Miz Galt puts in then. "We'll give you a receipt, all right and proper, but you wouldn't want to leave without no savings, was you to decide not to stay."

I might of knowed they'd be a catch in it, but I didn't feel like I ought to put up no argument, so I says, "Yes, mam."

"Nickel a week to spend and you'll get your candy whole-sale price," says she, giving me a look like she known what I was thinking and it seemed comical to her. I couldn't see nothing funny. Well, I'd have a quarter of a dollar ever five weeks, anyways. If I could keep from buying candy. And I hadn't had no candy in a powerful long time.

When they didn't neither of them say nothing for a minute, I says, "I could start in right now if you was to show me what I should do."

"Well," she says, "maybe this afternoon would be better, George. Strikes me it must of been a time since you had a hair-cut, and right now I think I'll take you out back and cut some off."

"Yes, mam," I says. I reckon I was pretty shaggy. Last time Milo'n me'd stopped off at a house, a farmer's wife had got after me with a shears, but that was a good while ago. I'd never of let her at me then if it hadn't been for Milo going first. I don't know why I purely hate a haircut so. Yet they ain't no way out of them excepting being bald, or wearing pigtails like a Injun or a girl.

"And that ain't the worst, George," Miz Galt says. "I wouldn't want you to say I'd snuck up on you unbeknownst. While I'm cutting, the water'll be heating on the stove, and when I'm through, you'll have to take a bath."

"I was swimming last week," I says, but I didn't say it loud, and I was looking at the floor. Just then a man come in the store, and she says, "Come along, George," so we went off to the kitchen once more.

They wasn't no use to struggle against her, so I give up and give in. First she set the kettle and a big pot of water on the stove; next she laid a old sheet on the floor and set the stool on it, then she wrapped a sheet round my neck so tight she like to choked me, and cut my hair. The clippings got inside my shirt just the same, like when the Old Crab done it. But Miz Galt, she didn't pull and tweak so bad, and she'd say something cheerful ever now and then besides just, "Hold still!" or, "Bend your neck!" She told how they was a swimming hole up back of town, with a grapevine swing over it, and how she'd show me the way over to it one afternoon when I got settled down, and when she says, "That's all!" and unpinned the sheet, I couldn't hardly believe she was done.

Next she taken a copper tub out from behind the stove and begun pouring water in it. All of a sudden I wondered did she think she was going to *wash* me too? *No!* thinks I, *a person's got to draw the line somewheres! I ain't going to let her, and that's that!* While she went off and come back with a towel and soap and a bundle, I stood there getting ready to fight for my rights. She opened up the bundle, and it was clothes.

"Put these on when you're done," she says. Then she closed the door to the back yard, went to the one leading into the hall, and went out, closing it after her. *That* was a relief to me!

I pulled down the blinds, in case somebody should come snooping around, turned the keys in both doors, and taken off my clothes. I noticed a bit of kindling just a good size for a boat on top of the wood box, so I put it in the tub and floated it round for a time. Finally I got in, washed, got out, dried, and put on the clothes. They didn't look like they was new, but they was a heap better than mine. I emptied out my old pants pockets to change em over and found a lot of things there I'd forgot I even had, I was just sorting em over on the kitchen table when she rattled the knob.

"George!" she calls. "Ain't you done yet? I got to get dinner on!"

"Yes, mam," I says, put the things in my pockets, and went and unlocked the door.

"Well, now," she says, "you look better, you smell better, and I bet you feel better!"

All the answer I give her to that was, "Can I help you to

112

empty out the tub, mam?" Women is never satisfied. She made me get clean, all right, but I couldn't see no reason for me to have to enjoy it, too.

26

So that was the beginning of the first day.

After dinner, in the afternoon, Mr. Galt showed me round the store where different things was kept, and later, Miz Galt taken me out to the barn and told me chores I was to do there. When supper dishes was done, she lit a lamp on the kitchen table, and we all set round while he put on his specs, got out a book, and read. It was somebody or other's essays, it said on the cover, and it was so uninteresting I couldn't tell you a word it said, yet I didn't know what to do but set there acting like I was listening; pretty soon I got such a fit of the gapes she noticed me and says, "Look's like somebody's ready for bed. Come along, George, I'll show you your room."

As it turned out, that downstairs bedroom where I slept first was the spare room; on the second story in the gable they was a little room acrost from theirs which she had fixed up for me. That first night, she taken me up to it and said goodnight, leaving me the lamp; I undressed, blown it out, and lain there feeling strange at where I was, how I got here, what would happen next, and all. I begun to think of Milo, wondering whether he was dead or alive; then I bawled, and then I was asleep; next day I got up and begun doing my chores, and before long it seemed like I'd been there quite a time.

Though my room was little, she'd fixed it nice, with a dresser, a bed, a chair, a rag rug, and two pictures on the wall. One of them wasn't but a text she'd worked—*Suffer the little children*—but t'other was a dandy one showing a shipwreck, with great waves and rocks and storm clouds; I'd lay in bed of a morning studying on it and wondering if any on board was saved (they wasn't no lifeboat I could see) or was all hands drownded, or if one feller was washed up on the shore of a desert island and found a cave, and all like that. Then after I'd hear the Galts had got up and was moving around, I'd get up, too, dress, and skin downstairs so's I could say I was all washed when she asked me—sometimes I was, too. And I'd see the wood box was filled, go out to the barn and pitch some feed down to the team if they wasn't out to pasture, throw corn to the chickens, and gather the eggs. When I was done, she'd have the breakfast on, and we'd all set down and eat. Mr. Galt'd say grace, but he weren't unreasonable about it—just "Bless, oh Lord, this food to our use and us to Thy faithful service," and you could pitch in. When breakfast was over, I'd go up front in the store with him and dust off the shelves with the feather duster even if they wasn't dusty; when Mr. Galt'd bring stock for the store back from town, he'd show me where it went and I'd put it away, until I got so I known where to stow it myself, and he didn't have to tell me no more.

Something I noticed from having traveled and lived all over like I done is this: after you been in a place a while, you can look back on the first time you come there, and it seems like it was another place altogether. Like at Galts—after I was there two-three days and found out how all the different rooms was placed and where things was and all, I would remember that first time I come out the downstairs bedroom, not even sure which way I should turn, and it didn't seem like it was the same house then as now.

It's the same with folks, or somewhat. Take Jim. That first time I come on him setting in the privy reading his book, I jumped like he was a hant, he struck me so queer. But later on, once I caught on to his ways and got talking to him and all, he just seemed natural, like I'd knowed him a long time. Same with Milo, in a different sort of way. The Galts was more gradual, though. You just come to know em slower, and you couldn't guess so easy what was on their minds. I couldn't tell if I was doing all right and they was planning on keeping me there or what.

I don't mind saying I liked her better than him. Neither one of them was what you'd call talkers, but it looked like he'd never use two words where one would do, and he'd never use one if he could show you instead. Like when I was learning my way about the store. When I'd have to ask where was so-and-so, instead of saying, "On the top shelf," or, "Behind the sugar barrel," he'd just step over and lay his hand on whatever it was. Then I'd wonder was I a fool for asking and should of seen it there myself, or was that just his way. I'd try to step around smart when I was in the store there, and see what I should do

114

before he'd ask me to do it, but I was never sure was I more nuisance or help to him. On the other hand, when I done something foolish and known it, he wouldn't bless me out the way you'd expect him to neither. I often wished he would. Looked to me like when the other feller don't call you a fool, you got to call yourself one, and it's worse.

Now Miz Galt would talk all right when she'd a mind to it, though I don't mean to say she'd any way talk you to death. She didn't mind telling you if you done a thing right, or if you done it wrong neither, and sometimes she'd get that look on her face like I was tickling her funny bone when I couldn't see why, which was just about the only times she'd make me mad. Why couldn't she just tell me I'd acted the fool and be done with it? Only then she'd usually say something so I'd have to laugh, too, so I couldn't stay mad with her long. Sometimes she'd set me to peeling potatoes or hulling peas while she was at the stove, and then she'd chatter along, telling different stories of when she was a little girl and such. She fell out a apple tree and busted her arm like I done falling out the loft that time. The right one, too, just like me. To hear her tell it, girls ain't so different from boys as you'd think. I could just about imagine her, littler, with her hair down, flying around kind of wild. Now, Mr. Galt, well, maybe it's harder to picture a bald-headed feller ever being a boy. I couldn't figure him ever cutting up or getting into monkey business or playing games, or so, though it stood to reason he must of growed up from something.

Folks coming in the store spoke to me sometimes, and some old tabbies would begin asking questions of me, like what my name was, where was my folks, and the usual. Them was times I was thankful to Mr. Galt, only I didn't know how to say so, because right away he'd think of something for me to do, to get me out of answering them. Boys and girls would come in, too, but they wouldn't do no more than stare and ask for what they wanted to buy. I didn't want to talk with them neither, so that was fine with me. And I stuck pretty close to the place so I didn't run into no one except in the store, until one warm afternoon Miz Galt says didn't I want to find my way over to the swimming hole. I says yes, so she told me the way, and I went.

I follered her directions and got there all right. When I found the spot, I was glad to find they wasn't a soul there but me. I taken my clothes off and had me a high old time, swinging on that grapevine and jumping off, kerplunk! where the water was deep. I swum down to the bottom and brought up some pebbles and a rusty horseshoe; once I spit water through my teeth clear from one bank to tother. Then I come out and was taking it easy in the sun when I heared voices coming pretty near; by the sound, I couldn't of got my clothes on or gone before they come if I'd wanted to, so I set there hugging my knees; pretty soon a bunch of fellers come along the path, five-six of them, some bigger and some littler than me; a big black-headed feller with a busted-off tooth in front, who talked like he known he was the kingpin, and behind him that fat red-headed feller I seen at the camp meeting and told me about the Reverend Spotts being kilt. I didn't feel much like staying there, but I didn't feel like running away, neither.

"Hi!" says the black-headed feller when he seen me. "It's the orphan from Galts'."

Then I stood up and looked at them all, but I didn't say nothing. I was waiting for that fat feller to speak up and say he seen me before, but he just stared like the rest. They all had their clothes on and I was bare-naked, which made me feel double queer.

"Where you from, orphan?" says the black-headed one, in a looking-for-trouble voice, and the rest of them laughed like they was something comical in that. I known they was going to be a fight, and I known I would get licked, but I hoped I could get my clothes on first and fight just one at a time.

"My name is George Mellish," I says, as ugly as I could. "Use it."

He looked kind of surprised, and says, "Is that so?" like I had him stopped for a minute. Then finally the fat feller hollers out:

"Hey, Lem, hey, Lem! I seen him before! He's a big lie! He ain't no orphan! He was to the camp meeting with his folks. He told me so hisself!"

"Galts is going to be murdered in their beds like the Reverend Spotts, taking in rag, tag, and bobtail, my ma says!" a little feller pipes up.

"Hoh!" says the black-headed one. "He ain't big enough to heft a ax! He looks too puny to lick St. Elmo here!"

Well, *that* I could of done, and for a minute I hoped it wouldn't be no worse, but then I knowed it was no use hoping —I might as well fight the big one, get licked, and be done with it.

"If I fight," I says, "it ain't going to be with no jelly roll like St. Elmo."

"Oh no?" says the big one.

"No," says I.

"Ain't he brave?" he says in a Miss Nancy voice, and the rest of them laughed. Then I begun to itch to take a crack at him.

"You going to give me a chance to put on my clothes or don't you dast fight fair?" says I.

"Put em on," says he, and I went and climbed into my pants and shirt, with them all staring at me. *I wish I never come here,* I thought. *Anyways, I don't have to stay. I'll fight him and then I'll get my pay from Galts and go on. I don't have to be no scarecrow for no one-horse town to mock at. Rag, tag, and bobtail, am I?* And I turned around and says, "Are you ready?" so quick I could see he was took by surprise, but he says, "Yes," put up his fists, and I went right in and punched his nose.

Well, we punched and cuffed and kicked and rolled around, and I was too busy fighting to remember much about how it went. The others was yelling and cheering, "Go it, Lem!" only once I thought I heard a voice say, "Hurray for the orphan!" when I landed one on his eye. He bloodied my nose, too, and I cut my fist on his broke-off tooth; once we rolled down the bank into the water and had to quit fighting until we clumb out; I could feel my one eye swelling shut, and I didn't have no more breath; finally he got me down and sat on my stomach till there wasn't nothing for it but to holler, "Nuff!" Anyways, I never bawled.

So he got off me and I got up; they was all jumping up and down and hollering and slapping him on the back like he was Jack the Giant Killer instead of half a head tallern me; I started off the way I come without looking at them, but when I heared that St. Elmo sing out after me, "Stay away from this here swimming hole, liar!" I faced round and hollers back, "I may be winded, but I can still lick you, fatso!" and this time it sounded like the laugh was on him, which made me feel some less miserable, but not much.

I went stumbling along the path, hurting in more places than one, only seeing out of one eye, with my shirt tore in half down the back and covered with blood down the front. Behind me, I could hear them yelling and splashing until I got too far away from there. *Well,* I thought, *I reckon that ends that. I'll go in her clean kitchen with the good clothes she give me all tore up, and I'll get my walking papers this time for sure . . .* Looked like the idea give me some kind of satisfaction, almost. If you can't get nothing to go right, you might as well enjoy it going wrong.

Hit the road again, thinks I, *that's what it'll be for me. Don't even know what's the next town the railroad passes through.*

I could of cleaned myself off some, but I reckoned I'd still look so bad there wasn't no use to try. When I got to the kitchen door, there she was, scraping carrots in the sink and humming to herself. She heard me before she looked up, and she says. "Well, now, how was your swim? Was they any other boys there?" thrown a carrot in a bowl of water, and turned her head towards me. "Oh my Lord! Oh, George!" she says, dropped the knife on the floor, and started towards me with her hands held out all dripping wet. Then she stopped short. "Oh," she says. "You been in a fight."

"Yes, mam," I says, and couldn't look at her no more.

"Well, set down," she says. "I'll get something to clean you off." So I set on the kitchen stool, and she went off without a word. Wasn't till then I begun to really feel bad. I could stand it if she'd scold me or lick me or anything, I thought, if only she wouldn't just say nothing but send me on my way without a word. Then she come back with some cloths and the arnica bottle.

"Take off your shirt," she says. "Just throw it on the floor. It ain't no more good but for rags." So I done it, she filled a bowl with water from the kettle, and begun to wipe my face. It hurt, but I just closed my eyes—the one that would still open, that is—and grit my teeth. I never looked in her face to see if I could tell what she was thinking, because I was afraid to find out. So I like to jumped out of my skin when I heard her start in to laugh.

"An eye gouged in and a ear chewed off, a half-mast tail and the whooping cough!" she says. "Who won?"

"He did," I says, and I didn't know which I was the most of, mad or relieved at her laughing that way.

"Who?" says she.

"Some big—some feller named Lem something."

"Lem Staple," she says. "Watch out, now, this'll sting." It did. "He's six inches taller and two years oldern you. But you couldn't be so bunged up if you hadn't give *him* something to remember."

"Bloody nose," I says, and when I recalled that first punch, I begun to feel better. "Maybe a loose tooth."

"That's a start," she says. "Next time he'll think twice before picking on you. But I guess a boy always has to fight his

118

way when he comes to a strange town. Girls will pick on a stranger, too, but in other ways. I hope it ain't discouraged you about staying, though, George."

I opened my good eye to look at her and says, "Oh no, mam, I ain't changed my mind! I'd like to stay."

"That's good," she says. "Now go put on your other shirt and do your chores."

And that was all they was to that, except for having a black eye for some time to come, and getting pretty sick of folks in the store asking me did I run into a door.

27

Ever night, after I got in bed, I used to think of Milo, and imagine he was alive somewheres, and would come back after me. I didn't know how he'd go about finding me, but I'd pass over that some way, and there he'd be one fine day; he'd tell me how he'd been obliged to leave me that time on account of having to flee from his enemies, but now he'd licked em all and didn't have to worry no more; how all the time he'd been keeping track of me, secret-like, and now he was ready to travel on together once more. And I'd tell him how I'd never forgot about him neither, and how I'd searched for him until there wasn't no place left to look. Then we'd go off again and have adventures and see the Pacific Ocean, and not be parted no more the rest of our lives.

After I went to sleep I'd dream of him often enough, too. Only the dreams wasn't like the stories I'd make up—more of them was awful, or sad. Sometimes they would be that he was dead, or fighting his enemies with me tied to a tree or some way not able to help him; sometimes he wouldn't even speak to me because he was still riled at me getting saved. Once I dreamed I found him setting fishing on the bank of a creek; I crept up behind him and grabbed ahold of his shirt so's I pulled it right out of his pants. I known I was dreaming, the way you do, sometimes, but I could just feel that shirt in my hand so plain that I yelled out, "Dream or no dream, this time I'll keep you!" Then before he even turned round, I woke up and found myself with a bunch of sheet in my hand where I thought the shirt would be . . . And once I dreamed he was with me, with everything just fine; he looked at me so straight and true, put his hand on my shoulder, and says, "Why, George, you and me is pardners—together we'll walk the world!" And when I woken up from that one, I cried.

Also, them dreams I used to have of the Fool Killer come back on me from time to time, all mixed up with the preacher being chopped up, and blood, and gore; sometimes it turned out 'twas me done the murder, and I'd wake up feeling terrible, like I'd really done it—only it was something else I done was wrong, and I guess I got to tell it now.

Galts done like they promised and give me my nickel ever week, along with a receipt for the twenty cents they banked for me. I kept them nickels under the paper of my dresser drawer, with the quarter I found in the road, and sometimes I'd get em all out to hold and count and chink against one another. For the life of me I couldn't decide whether when I'd saved up five I'd trade them in for a quarter so's I'd have two, or take the first quarter and the five nickels to trade for a fifty-cent piece. One time I'd decide one way, another time, another.

Then one day Miz Galt says to me, "George, don't forget you get your candy wholesale price at the store. I never saw a boy before didn't want to spend his money on candy!"

And I hemmed and hawed and says finally, "Yes, mam—no, mam—I been saving up—I ain't got much of a sweet tooth."

Which meant that besides having become a thief, I'd gone back to being a liar, too.

Because I'd been stealing candy right along.

They ain't no use to say I ain't ashamed to tell it, because I am. And you can believe me or not, I was ashamed when I done it, too, only it didn't stop me. I often wisht I'd had the chance to tell Milo about it and have him explain to me how a person could act so. But I never did.

The best I can say is something like this: I always did love candy, long as I can remember—jawbreakers and licorish and pepmint sticks and butterscotch and taffy—anything you can name. And I'd never before et my fill of it—never in my life. The Old Crab and the Old Man never bought none, that was sure, and it was only once in a blue moon back there when I was with them that I'd run a errand for some other folks and earn a cent, or once I found a whole nickel under the church steps.

When I went to work in the store, Mr. Galt says I was to wait on the children wanted candy; he told me how much was each kind, and showed me the kegs down underneath the counter which I was to fill the jars from when they got empty All the time he was explaining it, my mouth was watering so bad he must of noticed it, for he says, "Have a piece, George," and I says, "Thank you, sir," and taken a jawbreaker—green.

He never said nothing about not to take any without saying so, so, thinks I: *If I sell it to them others, why shouldn't I to myself?* Right off, I begun taking a piece ever now and then, but making a mark on a piece of paper ever time, so's at the end of the week I'd know how much I owed, and pay up.

But then, it must of been I took one more often than you'd think was likely, because when the end of the week come and I got my nickel, I added up the marker, meaning to pay for sure, and it was twenty cents. I mean twenty cents wholesale.

I put the marker in my pocket, and I thought: *I'll tell em to-morrow.* 'Twas my first week working for them and already I had run up a debt I couldn't pay. Course, they had the twenty cents belonged to me, but I'd agreed I wasn't to touch that until I left for good. And then, they was the quarter I picked up in the road. But some way I couldn't get myself to part with that until I couldn't think of nothing else at all. Like I said, I'd never had a whole quarter at once before.

I guess 'twas the night after that I begun to dream of the Fool Killer again, and woken in the night, tossing and turning. *Even if I give my quarter,* I'd think, *I can just see her thinking how much candy I ate, and laughing at me! It was a lot, I reckon, but, well, I ate it, and I can't see nothing funny in it . . . But worsen that, supposen they reckon they can't trust me no more if I buy on credit like that without telling no one, and they say, "We're sorry, but we think we'll look for another boy"? Then I'd lose my quarter and the job and not have nobody to travel with me no more and—it ain't fair! Other boys has folks buys them candy and clothes and keeps them till they're growed, and don't nobody say they got unusual luck! I never asked to be no orphan! I run away on my own hook, to be sure, but . . .*

Well, the upshot of it was, I got up then and there, in the middle of the night; taken the marker out of my pants pocket, tore it up in little pieces, chewed the pieces, and spit the wad out the window in the top of the maple tree, went back to bed and had bad dreams. And I never said nothing about the candy—just went on taking it—stealing it—with nobody noticing or saying nothing until she asked me why wasn't I buying none that day.

After that, I figgered I ought to be careful and not take none for a while . . . But that was the whole thing of it. I'd never of taken any at all if it hadn't been for having such a terrible hankering I couldn't stop myself . . . Oh, haven't you ever felt so—known you was doing wrong, but kept on doing it? And not only wrong. Wrong or wicked or sinful I could of stood easier. What about drove me crazy was knowing all the time what a blamed fool I was. Because I known the Galts was good to me; they fed me fine, and give me time off and never worked me to death; first she borryed them clothes for me, then she made some of my own out of his old ones cut down; this week they was talking of driving me over to town with him to buy me some brand-new shoes so's I could go to church with them—not that that'd be any treat. Another thing, sometimes of a afternoon, Miz Galt'd make doughnuts. Then she'd tell me to go get a good straight stick and clean it off. When I brought it in, she'd say take it in my fist and hold it up, and she'd drop warm doughnuts on it, right to the top . . . Why, I even took to saying my prayers at night without nobody telling me I should so's I could put Galts in the God-blesses along with Milo and my ma and pa which I'd never knowed . . . Yet there I was, robbing them all the while—and why? Because I had a sweet tooth. Wasn't no better answer. Well, if the Fool Killer wouldn't come for a person acting so, who'd he bother with at all?

But it didn't last long after that day she passed the remark about me buying candy . . . The time I usually done it was right after dinner, when Mr. Galt'd lay down on the parlor sofa for a snooze, and she'd be in the kitchen, washing up. After I'd got the hang of things, that was the time they'd send me up front to tend store by myself. Not many folks would come in that time of day; the store'd be shady and cool; I'd set in the rocker, dreaming about Milo, mostly, and ever now and then I'd sneak down by the candy kegs and take a piece. I might as well of took a handful in the first place. But each time I'd fool myself that this time would be the last.

Well, she caught me at it. I guess they was a wagon going by on the road, making a rattle so's I didn't hear her footsteps in the hall. The first I heard was her voice saying, "George." I had my hand right in the keg and my mouth full. I just froze.

"Are you buying that candy or taking it?" she says.

I dropped what was in my hand and straightened up, but I couldn't look at her, nor say nothing at all.

"I think you're taking it," she says. "I think maybe you been taking it quite a time."

"I——" I started out, but then they wasn't nothing more to say.

"Answer me, George. Is that true?"

I looked at her, then, and she was looking at me like that first time she caught me in the lie, with her eyes like rifle shots going right through. I couldn't say nothing, only nod and look at the floor.

"Go to your room and stay there," she says. "I won't say more until I thought what to do."

So I come towards her to go through the door, and when I passed her, I noticed the way she stepped back like she didn't want to have nothing more to do with me, which made me feel worse than anything.

I went up to my room and closed the door. Nobody come near me all the afternoon. I could hear folks' voices in the road, and footsteps and talking I couldn't make out down below me in the store; I wondered did she mean for me to do my evening chores, or stay there until I was told; I got out my nickels and my quarter and turned them over a little, like I was kind of saying goodbye, because I figgered I'd pay my debts before I left, anyways. Then I lain on the bed, looking at the shipwreck picture, and feeling miserable. I thought of that first time I run away, and I known that running away and being turned out is surely two different things.

Finally I heard footsteps coming up the stairs and acrost the upstairs hall. They was too heavy to be hers.

It's him, is it? thinks I, and all to once I was mad, for a lot of things, all mixed up in my mind. *He never gives a person the time of day; can't tell you if you done right or wrong; don't know if you're a human being or a ghost and don't care! Let him tell me to go! 'Twas her took me in and was good to me mostly anyways!* Then I jumped off the bed and taken the money in my hand.

"Here's your money!" I says, the minute he opened the door. "Don't need to tell me to go—I'm going! But I ain't no thief! I'm going to pay! I may be a orphan and rag, tag, and bobtail, but I ain't no thief! And you can keep the rest of what I earned, too! I got along before and I'll get along again! I don't need to be beholden to nobody!"

He just stood there, looking biggern usual, and it got awful quiet. Then he says:

"Put the money on the dresser."

I didn't want to, yet I didn't know what else to do, so I put it there.

Then he set down on the bed. "Lay over my knees," he says, and I known he was going to lick me, and he was a awful big feller, and I was scared.

"You ain't my pa!" I yells.

"Never said I was," says he. "Lay over my knees!"

"I won't!" I hollers.

"Oh yes, you will!" says he, and he taken hold of the back of my neck and bent me over as easy as a green twig. Then he held me down with the one hand while with the other, he walloped the daylights out of me. 'Tweren't but a hand licking, and I don't think it went on so terrible long, but I can't think of nothing to compare with it but getting kicked by a mule. I cussed and swore all the bad words I known while he was starting out, but at last I come to bawl. Finally he quit and let go my neck. I stood up. He taken a bandana handkerchief outen his pocket and handed it to me, saying, "Blow your nose." I blown, but I couldn't stop bawling yet.

He kept on setting. "Why did you do it?" says he.

That set me off blubbering worse. 'Twas enough to get a licking without a jawing, too.

"Quit carrying on," he says. "Why did you do it?"

I couldn't stop crying, but finally I says, "I—I never had enough candy before!"

"Why didn't you pay for it?" he says.

"I *said* I'd pay for it! I'll give you the money—you—you——"

"You wouldn't of if you hadn't been caught," he says. "Now you listen to me, George, and listen hard. Ever hot spell, candy melts and I lose moren you could of et in twice the time. I ain't worrying about the candy nor the money neither, because I just ain't that hard up. What I want to know is this. How did you feel when you was taking it?"

I didn't say nothing, nor look at him, just blown my nose once more.

"Maybe they's men can go on stealing and feeling right with thesselves at the same time, but from what I've seed of you so far, you ain't going to be that kind of a man. So you might's well give up the habit right now, because they ain't nothing in

124

the world you're going to want enough to make up for how stealing it will make you feel."

"It ain't a habit," I says, choking some. "I never done it before."

"Well," he says, and got up from the bed, "don't do it again. I'll say no more." And he went out the door and shut it behind.

Then I lain down on the bed (on my stomach) and reglar bellered. I couldn't even think of Milo, because I known even he'd be ashamed of me. I tried to think about the Fool Killer, and how maybe he'd come for me this time at last, but it seemed like that was when I finally known for sure that only a baby could believe in that tale. Because I'd almost of felt better if he *had* come after me, then and there.

I was bawling still when, after a long time more, footsteps come—hers, this time—and I heard her open the door. I just lain with my face in the piller and went on sobbing there.

"All right, George," she says. "You had the pleasure of feeling like a miserable sinner long enough. Set up and eat your supper."

I lain still, but the bawling stopped.

"Come on," she says. "You done wrong, you got licked, and that's that."

But I still couldn't move.

"Now listen, George," she says, "I see you're feeling sorry for yourself, but I hope you don't by no chance think I'm going to feel sorry for you, too. I'll tell you who I'm sorry for, which may come to you as something of a surprise. I'm sorry for Mr. Galt, because it ain't easy to give somebody a licking when you ain't angry and you ain't naturally mean, but because you think it's right. I seen him before he come up here, and I seen him after he come down, and he didn't look like he'd enjoyed himself no moren you. Now get up off that bed right now, *and I mean it!*"

I could tell she did, so I got up, handling myself kind of ginger, because, to tell the truth, I was sore.

Then she set down on the bed and says, "Turn round and take down your pants."

She still didn't sound like it was time for arguing, so I done what she said.

"Hmm!" she says, and laid her hand on the place, real gentle and cool. "I'm going to get some witch hazel and rub you off. That'll feel good." And then—there she was, off again. She began to laugh. "Oh, George," she says, "you really got a humdinger, now didn't you? That was a licking a boy could be proud of, it really was—I can see!"

Now here was the thing about the way she'd laugh at me. 'Twas always some kind of teasing so it would start off making me mad, yet there was always something in it—maybe just the catchy laugh she had—would get me going, too. What's there to laugh at in having your own tail warmed so's you can't set down easy for several days? Not a dad-burned thing! Yet she got me doing it, too—still half mad, but not able to stop it—till there was the two of us, laughing over nothing so awful funny *I* could see, until the tears run down.

"There!" she says finally. "Get your nightshirt on and I'll bathe your battle scars. Your supper's on the tray."

So I undressed while she went off for the witch hazel; she put it on and set with me while I et, telling me different stories of mischief she got into when she was a youngun; then she made me go to bed though it weren't but dusk-dark, and before she taken out the tray and the lamp, she leaned over to tuck me in, and kissed me on the cheek like a baby or a girl.

I didn't mind much at all.

28

That must of been about the time it stopped being late spring and started being early summer, and there wasn't much time between that and the end of what I got to tell, so let me see if I can recollect some of the things come between.

When I come in the store that morning after I got the licking, Mr. Galt kind of turned halfway round with his back to me, and I went for the duster, not feeling much like looking at him, neither. Then I heard him say:

"George, by and large you been doing satisfactory. From now on, anytime you want candy, just go ahead and take it without no charge."

When I sneaked a look at him, I seen the back of his neck all red, and I reckon my face was, too, but I says, "Thank you, sir," and went at dusting the shelves from top to bottom, as well as cracks I hadn't been into for weeks . . . The funny thing was, after that I seemed to of lost my sweet tooth, and it was a long time before I et any at all.

Somewheres along in there, Miz Galt asked would I care to call them Aunty and Uncle so's I would sound more at home, so I begun to do it, only it come harder with him until that licking kind of went out of my mind; whenever I could, I'd just call him You.

One day that St. Elmo come to the back door as bold as brass to ask did I want to go swimming with him. If it'd been me, I'd of been ashamed, but he acted like him and I had been the best of friends for a hundred years. I'd of told him no, I guess, excepting for Aunty being in the kitchen at the time and saying, "Go ahead, George." I was ready to fight again, if need be, but I didn't have to, in spite of Lem Staple being there with a bunch of fellers, some of which had been with him that day we had the fight and others I hadn't seen but in church or in the store. First off, nobody paid me much mind; later on, when we come out the water, we all played leapfrog, and I had a dandy time. When I come home, Aunty says, "What, all in one piece?" and I says, "Yes, mam."

Then it was most the Fourth of July, and they let Whiskey Pete out of jail.

Ever since I'd come to Galts', I'd been hearing of Whiskey Pete off and on. The Knights of the Soul Reborn never strung him up like they was planning on doing after the Reverend Spotts was kilt. Other folks at the meeting—"wiser heads," Aunty says—kept them from it and drove him over to the county jail instead. There he sot, waiting to come to trial; while he was in, he turned religious and got sanctified—the ladies said it was the preacher from our town brought it about by going to pray over him reglar; the menfolks thought 'twas more likely he went kind of loco from not being able to get a drink. But they wasn't nobody had much doubt 'twas Pete had kilt the Reverend Spotts, not only on account of having his still busted, but also because all could remember how one time he had the drunkard's fits and imagined they was a python round his middle squeezing him to death. A feller that crazy might do anything. That was why most everbody in town felt like you could of knocked em over with a feather when a peddler named Birdy Waters come round again on his circuit and went to court to swear to it he'd spent the night of the murder with Pete. They was drunk, to be sure, but Waters brought back another feller from over to Deepwell who'd been playing poker with them, too, up till the time they got too pie-eyed to see the spots on the cards, and that feller's wife also give witness, because of the poker game being held in her kitchen and over her dead body, pretty near. Anyways, the story stood up good enough so's they let Whiskey Pete free.

They was some says Pete could of stayed in jail another month without serving his time for all the things he'd never got caught at, while others believed 'twas the Lord's way of bringing him to the light, but most folks was up in arms to think a innocent man could be jailed that way, and the notion was got up of having some kind of celebration to welcome him back and show how all felt he'd been treated unfair. So the ladies of the church took over, deciding to get up a big supper at which the whole town would turn out; the mayor and the minister would speak, and Pete would get up to tell how he got saved by the Lord teaching him through adversity.

So when Pete got out of jail he went to stay at the minister's house, while the ladies got busy and decided on the T-shaped table instead of the horseshoe; the fried chicken instead of the stewed; if you went past the mayor's house, you could hear him practicing his speech out in the barn till his wife says he was making the hens too nervous to lay. The afternoon before the supper was to take place, all the ladies in town was cooking and frying and roasting and baking and collecting tablecloths and china and knives and forks; the girls was picking flowers and arranging em artistic, while the men and boys was doing their durnedest to keep out of the way so's they wouldn't be sent on a errand or set to work. In the afternoon, when I got off from the store, St. Elmo and Bill Bustard and me went moseying past the minister's house to see was Pete out and how was he feeling that day.

Sure enough, he was setting on the piazza, rocking as fast as a clock can tick, and he looked a miserable sight. The fellers said he used to have a beard, but it had been shaved off him in jail; his face was all white and pasty and sunk; his eyes was red, and he was hanging on to the arms of that rocker the way a person will grab the saddle on a bucking horse. Other days when we'd gone past and said howdy to him, he'd give us a kind of silly grin and said, "Now boys, mind your mas, and take the pledge if you haven't already done so," and Bill Bustard used to say if that was what taking the pledge done to him, he ought to give it back quick, because he used to be a gay old feller at one time. But today, when we give him a wave, he motioned us to come over near the piazza rail.

128

"Boys," he says in a kind of loud whisper, "boys, you got any human sympathy?"

Naturally we said we did.

"Boys," he says, "I been through a hard time. I been jailed unjust and I—do you know what they're making me do? Get up in front of the whole town to act like a blame fool tonight. How'd *you* like that?"

"Shucks, Pete," says Bill, "don't get cold feet. You'll do good."

Pete shaken his head. "They got no human sympathy," he says. "I got to get up there *cold sober!*"

"Naturally you got to be sober," says St. Elmo. "You taken the pledge, didn't you?"

"Oh hush up, St. Elmo," says Bill. "It's a shame, Pete."

"Boys," says Pete, "I known you had human sympathy. I known you had Christian charity. Now I don't suppose———"

"Don't suppose what, Pete?" asks Bill.

Pete leaned over in the rocker and looked both ways, up and down the road. "You know the old icehouse?"

We all nodded yes.

"Straight through the door. Straight through to the back. Turn to the right. In the corner, under a heap of sawdust. Buried pretty far down. A jug. Oh Lordy, boys, could you bring it here? I ain't been able to get out of their sight!"

Well, I don't know how you could of missed hearing about Pete being so spifflicated by the time he got to that supper that he just laid his head down in a bowl of potato salad and went to sleep in the middle of the mayor's speech. But it was never told before how the liquor got to him—not by Bill, nor me, nor even St. Elmo; to any thinks we done wrong, though, I say it was a act of mercy, not a crime. But, sorry as I was for the poor old buzzard, I had to laugh fit to bust when I first seen him laying there with his head in the cut-glass bowl like it was a goose-down piller; I couldn't stop laughing all the way home, and even Aunty and Uncle chuckled some after we got out, though they acted real sober and sorry saying goodnight to the minister's wife.

'Twas only after I was in bed with the light out and starting to get the stomach ache that it commenced to worry me. I begun to think how mad them church ladies was, and how much madder they'd be was they to find out who brought Pete the jug. And I thought how Bill's and St. Elmo's mothers was bound to say 'twas me had led their darling boys in trouble, me being a stranger and a orphan and nobody knowing nothing about me.

Next I wondered whether, if Aunty and Uncle was to find out who was to blame, they might look at it that I'd shamed them in public—in spite of thinking it was comical before they known who done it—and decide 'twas too much for them to keep me on no more.

I begun to sweat and toss and wish I hadn't et so much—fried chicken and ham and potato salad and pickles and hot rolls and three kinds of pie. Finally I dropped off to sleep, but it must of been the stomach ache and the worrying together give me such terrible dreams.

I can get scared just thinking of them, yet the funny thing is I can't remember in any clear way what they was, only they was blood in them, and folks chasing me with me not able to run, or I was trying to call out but couldn't make a sound—or so I thought, for, next thing I known, Aunty was shaking me, saying:

"Hush, George, stop your yelling! You just been having a dream."

Even then I couldn't shake it off, and I remember hollering, still kind of half asleep, "Don't let em get me, Aunty, don't let em near!"

"Ssh! Course, I won't! Ain't nobody after you. You're right here in your own bed."

I grabbed hold of her hand and pulled her down to set beside me. I could see her by the light of the candle she'd set on the washstand, in her wrapper, with her hair down in a braid. "Don't go way, Aunty!" I says. "Stay here, please!"

"I'm not going," she says. "They's nothing to fear."

And then—I don't guess I'd of said it except for being half asleep still, and not knowing whether I'd altogether got out of that dream—I says, "Aunty, don't send me away! You don't need to pay me no wages! I know I don't do right all the time, but don't send me away!"

"George!" she says. "Is that what you got on your mind?"

"I don't—you said it was for a trial when I come, and—I mean, I just ain't ever sure if it's all right."

I seen her look away from my face and kind of close her lips together. Then she taken her hand away and put it tother side of me on the mattress, to lean on. Her pigtail hung forward over her shoulder, and I taken hold of the end of it, so's to feel a piece of her still.

"George," she says, "you make me feel purely ashamed."

"I don't mean to, Aunty," I says. "I can't see that you got no call to be ashamed."

I was more awake now, and the dream was going away; if it'd

been day, I'd of felt foolish for kicking up sich a fuss, but laying in bed at night with only the candle, it looked like it was easier to say things than in the day.

"You got a right to let me go if I ain't suited you. I looked out for myself before. It's only I'd like to know for sure."

"George!" she says. "George, stop it! Listen to me, child, I been afraid to let on how much I *wanted* you to stay for fear you'd think I wasn't but a mushy female trying to hold on to you!—Ouch, child, don't pull my hair!"—for the way it made me feel to hear that, I must of give her braid a jerk.

"Excuse me," I says, and let up, though I didn't let go.

"You see, George," she says, kind of slow, "they's certain things you couldn't know."

After she stopped a minute, I says, "Like what things, Aunty?"

"Well," she says, looking away, "a long time ago, Mr. Galt and me had a baby, but it died."

"Oh," says I.

"And then it looked like the Lord didn't mean to send us no more . . . Don't nobody but Mr. Galt know most of this, George, and I don't know as I've even said it to him in so many words."

"I wouldn't tell nobody, Aunty."

"I know you wouldn't, George."

We was talking real low, and everthing else was still, except for once in a while you could hear a half-asleep chirp from some bird, and then a big June bug come buzzing in the winder after the candle, batted against the walls, and, by luck, found the winder and flew out again.

"I just want to give you a idea of how things was before you come along. 'Twas right after the camp meeting, remember?"

I'd never forgot.

"I'd never got over wishing I had a family, George. Mr. Galt was disappointed, too, but it looked like he could go on about his business and not dwell on it so much. I guess women is more apt to make thesselves miserable over such things."

She stopped again, and finally I says, "I guess so."

"When the camp meeting come round this year, I persuaded Mr. Galt into taking me over there. We was never camp meeting folks. Never looked to us like all that hollering and carrying on was the right way to worship. Only this time I'd got to thinking—I don't know's I can explain—I wondered if maybe we'd been too stiff-necked and high and mighty and could that of

131

been a reason why—well, a person gets notions sometimes. Anyways, it was my doing we went.

"And then they was that awful killing, after which we come home. Even before it, I didn't feel nothing but plain disgusted at the whole monkey show."

I wondered if I should tell her I'd got saved, but I decided to keep still.

"Mr. Galt and me never mentioned it to one another, but I felt like I'd acted foolish, getting him to close up the store and all to go, and I made up my mind then to try to leave off fretting so much over what I hadn't, and try to give more thanks for what I had.

"Then you come along. You come in the store just like any other boy, only you was a stranger, and I found out you was by yourself, without no folks and all." She taken away her hand she had been leaning on, folded it with t'other one in her lap, and set up straight. "What I'm trying to lead up to in a round-about way is how a lot of things all together, and not all of them sensible, made me think how maybe you was sent to me, and maybe I'd be able to keep you, for mine. I know it *ain't* sensible, George, because I got no right to you, but so far as you leaving goes, I shouldn't be surprised if it would be a deal harder on Mr. Galt and me than on you. Mr. Galt don't say much, but that don't mean he don't feel it, too."

She was quiet again, while I felt like I was going to bust, and couldn't of spoke if I'd tried. The candle flame ducked and shivered with a wind come in the winder, and Aunty says, "Law, George, it's most dawn! Can you go to sleep now?"

But I still couldn't say nothing, so I just taken hold of her and pulled her down and hugged her hard.

THE FOOL KILLER
29

One day Uncle come back from town with a hound pup. He says him and me was to go pardners in it; when fall come, we'd take it out to hunt. He asked me to think up a name, so, after con-

132

sidering some of the usual ones like Rover and Fido and Tray, I says:

"Less name him Ulysses S. Grant, after the president."

Uncle says so long as the dog didn't read the papers he didn't reckon that would harm him none, so we went ahead and called him Ulysses for short, and teached him to answer to that name. Uncle shown me how to train him: with a string tied to his collar and a bite of meat to coax him, feeding him when he come to my call at the beginning, and then just petting and praising him after he begun to catch on. Aunty and me got him housebroke between us without too much damage to the carpeting. He was a smart pup, and the first I ever had—even a share of, I mean.

One afternoon, Ulysses and me went over to Bill's house to see did he want to go fishing, but his ma said he'd been in mischief and was being kept in. Then we went to St. Elmo's, but they wasn't nobody home there at all, and the shades was drawed, which made me remember they'd all gone to a funeral over to town. I could of chased up somebody else, but I decided I'd fish by myself and when I was through mosey down by the swimming hole where they was always bound to be company of a hot afternoon.

I went in the woods heading for a spot upstream from the place where we swum. I cut me a pole; I planned on digging worms out the bank; and I had my line and hooks in my pocket, like always. (Aunty was forever warning me about how one day I'd set down careless and *then* I'd see, but I'd explain to her how it's back pockets you got to watch for, not side.) Ulysses was quartering back and forth with his nose to the ground, businesslike as a growed dog; then he disappeared in the underbrush where I lost sight of him—but I didn't worry, because he was a smart pup, like I said, and I known he'd catch up.

Well, he didn't catch up—didn't need to, because when I got to the stream he was there ahead of me, and what had him interested was a man setting on the bank fishing just the way I was fixing to do. The man had his hand under Ulysses' collar and was scratching his neck, right there where you know it feels good, and when I laid eyes on him, I stopped stock-still.

I couldn't see but the back of him: the back of his head and how his ears was set onto it, the way he held his shoulders, and the little goldy hairs on the back of his hand shining in the sun —'tweren't enough to be sure—I couldn't say I knowed—only my heart begun to swell up and thump; I could feel myself getting hot and most likely red, because—oh, I could of wagered it was Milo! I could of swore!

Then he turned his head to say something to the dog—and it was him

"Milo!" I says, only my voice got stuck in my throat.

He heard me anyways, and turned right around. Then he got up, slow and easy, in that lanky man's way of his, and stood there just staring at me. It was like so many times I'd pictured it when I was awake, or dreamed it when I was asleep. Not hardly knowing which I was, awake or asleep, with my heart going like a drum, I says:

"You come for me!"

But it got more like I was asleep, not awake, for he never answered me; just stood there with his hands hanging down, staring, until I felt scared.

"Milo!" I says, real loud this time.

Then finally I seen him begin to smile, in amongst his beard. "George!" he says. "Why, it's George!" and the way he said it, it sounded like he'd been asleep a long time, and I'd only just woken him up.

At that, I couldn't stand it no more; I run at him and thrown my arms around his middle; my face was in his shirt and I smelled of his smell; I can remember thinking: *It can't be a dream because they ain't no smells in dreams!* "Milo! Milo!" I kept saying, while he patted my back, and Ulysses run around us in circles, barking.

Finally I dast let him loose; I backed off some, still holding to his arms, and I says, "Milo, where you been all this while?"

"Oh," says he, "hither and yon, like always."

"But, Milo," I says, "where did you *go?*"

"North for a time," he answers.

"I don't mean that," I says. "I mean where'd you go after the meeting? What happened to you?"

"What meeting?" says he.

"Why, the *camp* meeting!"

But he just looked at me, shaking his head. I was reasonable sure I was awake, yet it seemed queerer than any of my dreams.

"When I found the blanket all bloody and all, I thought maybe you was dead," I says. Still he didn't answer. "Or that maybe you was mad with me and didn't want me no more."

Then he put his hand up to pass it over his face like brushing away a cobweb, and I noticed his scar. I'd forgot how sharp and red it looked, running acrost his forehead and into his hair. Finally he spoken: "Oh no. I wasn't mad. Maybe—I don't know."

134

Oh, but he sounded queer, and it all come back, what I'd half put out of my mind: how he'd forgot the whole beginning of his life, how he'd had the spell that time and all, and I cries, "Milo, Milo, you ain't forgot *me?* You couldn't! You known my name!"

He smiled again, and his face stopped looking so odd. "Sure not, George," he says. "I couldn't of forgot you. You and me was good companions, wasn't we?" And he put his hand on my shoulder like I could remember he done one time in a dream.

Only this time it made me feel just cold, all through and through, and I says:

"You mean you ain't come back here for me?"

He says, "Why, George, if I'd of known——"

Then Ulysses got tired of not having nobody pay him no mind, I guess, and stood up on his hind legs with his front paws against me, commencing to whine. I was glad. I was thinking: *He forgot me! He forgot me! 'Twasn't his enemies—'twasn't even that he was mad!* And all the while I was petting Ulysses and saying, "Ain't he a beauty? His name is Ulysses S. Grant. He's six months old and he's half mine."

Milo taken his hand off my shoulder and squatted down to pet him, too. "Yessir," he says, "he's a likely pup. Who owns the other half?"

"Uncle," I says. "That's Mr. Galt. Galts is the folks taken me in after——" Then I couldn't say nothing for a minute, and neither did he. "Uncle runs the store. Him and me is going hunting with Ulysses, come fall. He'll be a little young, but it'll give him a chance to learn."

Milo stopped petting Ulysses and just squatted there, letting him lick his hand. I couldn't see but the top of his head.

"Milo," I says, "come on back and meet them. They're awful nice folks. You'll like them fine."

He didn't say nothing, nor move.

"Aunty—that's Miz Galt—she's just grand. She makes doughnuts and gives me a whole stickful. Uncle is a quiet sort of feller, but he's *fair*. He licked me once, and I was down on him for a time, but I got over it. I guess I had it coming to me. Come on back and meet them, Milo. Aunty'd be proud to have you for supper, I know."

He says, "No."

"You wouldn't have to stay the night if you didn't want. Just come and eat and come back here to camp, or sleep in the loft in the barn."

He didn't answer this time.

"Anyways," I says finally, "I got your other blanket and your knapsack belongs to you. Don't you want em back again?"

He raised his head and looked at me, then he stood up and looked down.

"Does that mean you ain't coming with me?" he says.

Now I told you what I'd been making up and dreaming of all this while: how he'd come back and get me one day; how we'd go on like we done before—eating when we was hungry, sleeping when we was tired, talking to folks when we felt like it and not when we didn't, like he used to say. Clear on out to the Pacific Ocean we'd go, and never be parted no more—that was how I'd pictured it—different parts ever single night before I'd went to sleep—and prayed for it, too. And when I first seen him, that was all the thought I had—of how he'd come for me, just like a wish come true.

Only now, with him standing right there in front of me asking me wasn't I coming—all I felt was my stomach kind of going down.

"Milo——" I says, "Milo, it ain't the same. What I mean, Galts ain't like the Old Crab and the Old Man, or Fanshawes. I couldn't just run away from them when they been so good to me. No moren I could do it to you." Only how could I stop from thinking: *Didn't he do it to me?* "If I was to leave, I'd have to tell em I was going, fair and square. And they'd like to see you, I know, Milo. They wouldn't try to stop me. They never asked me no questions much when I come, or tried to send me back nowheres. They just . . . Anyways," I says, and all of a sudden I had all I could do to keep from bawling, "I couldn't take Ulysses with me. He's half Uncle's, and he'd be sure to foller if I was to go now."

"All right," he says, "go on, then." And his face was so I couldn't tell what he meant.

"Oh, please, Milo!" I begs him, grabbing his arm, "come back with me! If you known them you wouldn't want me to do them so! Please come and——" But if I'd of said any more, I'd of bellered for sure.

He pulled his arm away, but he says, "All right. If you want me to so bad, I'll come, but I ain't coming with you now. You better go on back and tell them first. I'll be along after."

Then I had another awful feeling inside me that he didn't mean it and I'd never see him again, and I reached out and clutched at him. "You promise? Cross your heart and hope to die you'll come soon?"

"I promise," says he.

"You don't even know where the house is!" I says. "You don't mean to come at all!"

But he shaken me off like I was a fly, and says, "You said it's the store, didn't you? Didn't you hear me give my word?"

I couldn't remember he'd ever spoke to me so cold and mean, and it made me feel worse than ever, but I didn't know what else to do, so I says, "It's the last house on the east end—it ain't like you really had to go *in* the town. Come soon, Milo!"

"I'll be there," says he.

Then I turned and walked off, with Ulysses after me, and my heart further down in my boots ever step of the way.

30

They'd been plenty of times before when I'd thought of telling Aunty and Uncle of all the things had happened to me up to when I come to live with them. But some way, the right moment for it had never seemed to come along. For one thing, they was folks was always busy at something or other, and when I was around they kept me pretty busy, too. For another, they was the least nosy folks I ever seen—they'd never ask me no questions to get me going, and though I'd often just about have my mouth open to start in telling—like on some of those days Aunty'd be talking of when she was a girl—I don't know why, but I never could seem to begin.

Now the time had come when I would have to, and it looked to me like it was the worst time in the world.

Because I could tell about Milo and me meeting up, and all about his strange story, and the camp meeting, and losing him, and all that, odd as it was—but how was I to tell Aunty or Uncle of him asking me to travel on? And I couldn't tell the one thing without the other, could I now?

I was walking along thinking so much I wasn't paying no attention to where I was going; just then I stumped my toe on a rock so hard I like to busted it. It made me cuss and swear, but I was almost glad to have it hurt me so.

When I come to the kitchen door, they wasn't nobody inside. I reckoned she'd be in the store or upstairs sewing, but I didn't feel like looking for her just then. Instead, I went in, set down to the table, and put my head on my arms. Not to bawl. Just to shut my eyes and not see nothing for a while.

Milo could live here, I thinks. *They's the spare room. Aunty and Uncle'd let him, I bet. He could be a blacksmith, or hire out for any kind of hand. Even if he was afeared of living in the town on account of his enemies, couldn't he camp out a ways? Or if he'd build a place of his own off from the town, that wouldn't be a strange house. And I could visit back and forth between him and Uncle and Aunty different times.*

Only I known that would never come true. Milo and me used to talk of building us a cabin by the Pacific Ocean after we got West and settling down there to fish and hunt and watch the waves roll in, but, setting there thinking of it, I had my doubts we ever would. Seemed to me Milo just wasn't the kind would ever want to stop roving—if I was with him, I'd keep going on, long as they was any place left to go.

And it appeared to me like I'd got soft or something. I'd got so I *liked* living in a house and sleeping in a bed and feeling like I belonged somewheres. Why, I even liked working! It make me feel kind of big and important when folks would come in to ask for this and that at the store, and I'd know right where it was on the shelf, and how much it cost, and all.

Then, though course I known it was true what Milo said about you didn't need money to have you a good time, it only made me wonder all the more was Aunty just about right when she used to tease me for turning into a miser. Because between the quarter I'd found, and my cash earnings from the store, and a few odd jobs I done for old Miz Arbuckle hadn't no man to help her out, I was only five cents short of enough money to change in for a silver dollar—whole! I known I ought to be ashamed for thinking of that now, but I couldn't hardly stand to think of not getting it when I'd come so close.

Then I heard her footsteps coming down the hall, but I didn't have the gumption to move from the way I was setting there.

"George!" I heard her say. "What's the matter? Don't you feel good?"

I set up then, and, without looking at her, I says, "It ain't that. I ain't sick or nothing. It's just—I got something to tell you."

She set down in the chair acrost from me and give me a grin,

138

but I didn't smile back. "Tell away!" she says. "Just don't scare me to death looking like the world's coming to a end!" But some way I still couldn't begin. "I'll get you started," she says then. "You been in some kind of mischief?"

"No, mam," I says. "Not as I know."

"Where's Ulysses?" she says. "Ain't nothing happened to him?"

But just then he wandered in the back door with his tail wagging, and went nosing up to her like he heard his name.

"Merciful heavens, don't keep me in suspense, George! Out with it!"

I wished she wouldn't josh me right now. It made it more hard to commence. But finally I did.

"When I come here, Aunty, you never asked me no questions about where I'd been or what I'd done, after you found out I hadn't no kin nor nobody cared about me."

I was looking at her now, and I seen her face change. She didn't look like laughing no more.

"I always meant to tell you on my own accord," I says, "only they was so many different things, and——"

I kind of run down, so she says, "Never mind. I known you'd tell me what you wanted in your own time."

"Well," I says, "just before I come to live with you, I was traveling with a feller. That is, I was up until the camp meeting. That was where I lost track of him. We'd met up along the way a time before when I was running away from—well, Aunty, it ain't that I wouldn't be glad to tell you about that, too, only it's kind of long."

"Go ahead, George," she says. "Just tell it your own way."

"This feller's name was Milo Bogardus," I says. "I mean that's what it still is. Only it ain't rightly his own name at all, because it was took off a dead feller and give to him. And all this time I thought *he* was dead, too, or anyways I weren't sure, until this afternoon . . . Oh, Aunty, I just know you'll like him fine!"

"Course, I will, George, if he's your friend and was good to you."

"Oh, he was awful good to me—the best of anybody I ever known—excepting you and Uncle! And he's a interesting feller, too, on account of having such strange things happened to him in his life!"

But then it looked like I was stuck once more.

"Just start in anywhere with what you got to say, George. I'll piece it together, and ask you if it ain't clear."

So then it all come tumbling out, one thing on top of another, and some things backwards, I guess: how Milo got wounded and forgot about everthing had ever happened to him in his life before; how him and me met up and traveled along together; how he had the spell that time and give me such a fright, but then he got all right again and weren't no different from before; how we come to the camp meeting and he didn't want to stay but I persuaded him by promising him not to get saved, and then went ahead and did; how I woken up next morning and found him gone—the morning they found the Reverend Spotts kilt—how I went off in the fields to look for him but never found nothing in most a week except that blanket covered with blood . . . But in all of it, I kept back about how Milo known he had enemies in strange cities and strange houses, because I had always knowed that that was the really secret thing he told me and trusted me never to say . . . And also, they was something inside me wouldn't let me tell how odd he was when I found him by the stream this time, how he seemed like he'd clean forgot about me at first. I wished I could tell it, but it looked like I just couldn't get it out.

Aunty listened and listened all the while I went on, with her face looking more solemn ever word, but not interrupting at all.

When I was done, she says, "But, George——" Then she stopped and begun over. "And now he's come to take you away!"

Her voice sounded so sad and serious as I couldn't hardly stand; yet it was the truth she said, and they wasn't nothing I could answer; all I could do was stop looking at her and say, quick as I could:

"I told him to come here, Aunty. I told him I known you'd ask him to stay to supper. Was that all right?"

"Just right, George."

"I wanted you and him to meet up with one another—oh, Aunty, you and Uncle will like him fine! He's got all kinds of sensible ideas, like——" *like folks going naked more* was what come to my mind, but I decided against it "——like he don't care for camp meeting kind of religion no moren you!"

She pushed her chair back from the table and got up from it slow, like she was feeling tired.

"Course, we'll like him, George. Don't you worry about that. Now I believe I'll go and tell Uncle we're having company for supper." But she didn't move, just stood there staring at the floor, pushing the hairpins in her knot. "And since we are, I guess I'll ask you to kill a chicken for me." Then finally she went out, down the hall towards the store, leaving me setting there—which was when I really did bawl.

Afterwards, I went out and catched me a pullet and chopped off its head—a job I purely hate most days, but right then I taken it as kind of a relief—I even scalded it and begun plucking without being told. Aunty come back from the store while I was at it and says:

"Why, George, that's a good boy! But I'll just take over on that now so's you can tell Uncle what you just told me."

Uncle was behind her, though it wasn't quite closing time; him and me set down at the table while she worked, and I told all about Milo and me again. When I was done, Uncle says, "Hm," and not another word.

Then Aunty says, "Go out to the springhouse and bring me a crock of butter, George," and when I went out I catched sight of Milo in the distance. I could tell it was him by that long-legged walk of his, cutting over the fields.

31

So after I brought Aunty the butter, I run out to meet him; he give me a wave when he seen me coming; when he come near me, he smiled and put his hand on my shoulder while we walked along together, the way he used to do. Then he didn't seem so odd no more, and I kind of loosened up inside, even though we wasn't saying nothing.

When we come to the back yard, Aunty was standing in the kitchen door with her hand up shading her eyes; she says, "Howdo, Mr. Bogardus; Mr. Galt and me is mighty pleased you could come to supper," and Milo says, "Howdy, mam," and I didn't need to say nothing at all. Uncle come out, and him and Milo shook; for a minute I felt like Ulysses and me was two of a kind, standing there while the rest of them talked, turning our heads from one to another but not real sure what was going on. Finally Aunty says, "Well, my goodness, I don't mean to keep you standing out here. Won't you step inside?"

Uncle says, "Nemmind your chores this evening, George, I'll

take care of em," but I answers, "Couldn't I take Milo along with me to show him round while I do em?" and Aunty says, "Of course, if you like." So I says, "Come on, Milo," and pulled him down towards the barn. He stood round while I fed the chickens; he led out Queenie to water when I taken Ned, he stood leaning against Ned's stall while I pitched down hay; he asked how come the team wasn't out to pasture in summer, and I explained how Uncle had to get up early tomorrow to go to town and didn't want to be bothered catching em in the morning; he asked how come we hadn't no cow, and I says it's because the folks next door kept em and we could get all the milk and butter we wanted there. When I was done, it seemed like didn't neither one of us want to go inside; Milo says, "Think I'll have me a pipe," and we leaned up against a sawhorse while he lighted up. It smelled wonderful. Uncle never smoked nothing at all.

After we was there a time without saying nothing, Milo says, "I seen Lake Michigan," and I says:

"Where's that?"

"Up north," he says. "It's the biggest lake you ever seen."

"Like the ocean?" I asks.

"Moren anything else. Sand bottom all the way acrost, so it's just as blue, and out a ways, they's a drop-off so the water goes from light blue to dark blue as sharp as if 'twas painted with a brush."

"That sounds like something I'd admire to see," I says.

"They's great forests, too, and flowers called Injun pipes growing round the roots of the trees that's dead white all over—white's a candle—stems, leaves, and all."

"We ain't got those round here," says I.

"A good many Injuns lives around there, too, but they ain't ugly. I lived with them for a time."

"You *did?*" I says. "In a wigwam and all?"

"Well, no," says he, "I just camped alongside."

"Did they have any scalps they'd took, left over from before they got quietened down?"

"They never showed me none, but they might of. They mostly make baskets and have gardens and hunt."

"With bows and arrows?"

"Lots of em has rifles, now."

"How do they talk? Injun language, or like us?"

"Some of both. They known some English and I picked up some of theirs, and we patched out the rest making signs."

"Say something in Injun language, Milo!"

142

So he says something didn't sound like anything, and says, "That means 'big house by the water.' "

Then neither of us said nothing right away, and what I was thinking was how I didn't have much of anything to tell him that I'd done. I mean, I'd been busy all right, working in the store, or swimming, or moseying around with Bill and St. Elmo and t'other boys, but I just kept doing the same ever day, and Aunty and Uncle, too, but Milo—why, living the way he done, you never known what'd happen next—see Lake Michigan or live with Injuns, or anything!

Finally I says, "Where you went was most as good as going West."

He knocked his pipe out on the floor and says, "Places is all alike except for the things you see in them," which made me recall the way Milo used to say things to me I couldn't see the sense of. Ain't that what people travels to different places for— to see different things in em? But Aunty called us in to supper then.

We washed up and set down to the table, Aunty at one end, Uncle at t'other, with Milo and me on each side. Uncle said grace, and for a time after, it was just *Please pass the this,* or *Won't you have some of the that?* until we got ourselves helped. Then we was busy eating for a while, but finally I begun to wonder if 'twasn't time to think of some remark to make. But Aunty started in to talking then; she says:

"I reckon you see a great many interesting things, traveling about the way you do, Mr. Bogardus."

Milo says, "Yes, mam, sometimes I do."

"Now me," she says, "I always had a hankering to visit Chicago, but ever time it looks like I might have the chance, something or other comes up. You ever been there?"

He says, "No, mam."

I started to say how Milo never went in cities or towns, but I changed my mind.

"Mind you, I wouldn't want to live there," Aunty says. "I'd just like to have a look at it and come back home. All them horsecars and operys and carriages and gaslights and folks dressed fit to kill—I'd just like to take a look at them once and then come home and have em to think of from time to time."

Milo says, "You got things all about you here that them folks never even heard of," and Uncle nodded his head. Aunty says, "Why, I never thought of it that way, but that's true!" and I felt good. But then it got kind of quiet again.

Aunty says, "Even in a little town like this we get some ex-

143

citement once in a while, of course, though it don't take much to make a nine-day wonder here. Somebody's cow has twin calves, or a girl you'd give up for a old maid gets married."

I thought of Milo, traveling round and living with Injuns and all, and it didn't seem like that could sound like much to him, so I puts in, "Well, Aunty, they was the Fourth of July, and the church supper for Whiskey Pete and all."

Aunty thrown back her head and laughed. "Oh law, yes! Did George tell you of that, Mr. Bogardus?"

Milo says, "No, mam."

So Aunty set out to tell of how Pete was let out of jail, and everbody was all ready to set him up for a reglar Christian martyr, when he got hisself pie-eyed and disgraced the church ladies—"Right in a bowl of potato salad, sleeping like a baby!" she says.

Then, to my surprise, Uncle opens up and says, "Well, now, Louisa, looks to me like you left out the real excitement when we had a murder happen not ten miles off, and nobody knows to this day who done it."

Aunty says, "Now Mr. Bogardus surely heard about that!"

But Milo shaken his head no, with his eyes shifting back from one of them to the other, quick as a bird's. And I got a funny feeling like I ought to say something to get the talk going another way. What if it come out how Milo was there at the camp meeting but didn't remember a thing about it? He taken it so queer when I brought it up before. Only I couldn't think what to say, and Aunty was already started, telling how the camp meeting was held over to Tucker's Grove the beginning of ever summer, and how she'd never thought any good come of folks getting stirred up and carrying on that way, yet they was no denying some seemed to get great good out of it, and this year her and Mr. Galt had even gone thesselves. I noticed Milo stopped eating, and so did I.

Then she told of how the Reverent Spotts was found kilt, with his own ax laying by him, and how most folks had been sure it must of been Whiskey Pete done it, mad because of his still being broke up by the Knights of the Soul Reborn, yet, still and all, the proof had come out he was somewheres else at the time, so it couldn't of been him after all.

And my heart commenced to beat fast, remembering that day when Milo was gone, and I found his blanket bloody and all; how it was a secret about his enemies, and I just busted out with the first thing come in my head.

144

"You know who I think done it?" I says, and they all looked at me.

"Who?" says Uncle, and I says:

"The Fool Killer!"

"Why, George!" says Aunty. "Who's that?"

Now for a long time I'd got over thinking of the Fool Killer excepting as a tale made up to scare babies with. Oh, Jim never meant to scare me—he was just a funny old man liked to tell tales like they was true—or, for all I know, he was so old he'd got things mixed up in his head so's he didn't know what was true hisself. I just said that to be talking, so's it wouldn't come out how Milo forgot the camp meeting, or had enemies he had to watch out for, or something. But now, it seemed to me like I had to kind of make out I'd meant it, so I started in telling it again the way Jim told me, and while I was telling, it even begun to sound kind of likely.

Because look how it all fit in: there was all them folks got together to carry on like a bunch of fools, shouting and jerking and speaking in tongues so's they'd of been carried off to a lunatic asylum if they'd done it any other wheres—why, St. Elmo told me once how he'd seed a bunch of growed men and women down on their hands and knees barking like a pack of hounds around a tree, thinking they'd got the Devil treed there!—and then, who was the ringleader of the whole kit and kaboodle? The preacher! Begging folks to repent and get saved, to be sure, but doing it by exhorting and shouting hisself, and egging em on to do it in a way surely looked foolish to sensible folks—Aunty and Uncle and Milo, for three. Then, look at the way he was kilt—chopped with a ax. Didn't that just about fit with the Fool Killer chopping fools? Course, the Fool Killer carried his own chopper around, but still—well, I got so wound up I come near convincing myself by the time I was through. Looking back, I can see now how Jim might of got so he believed his own tales.

I guess I must of been talking kind of fast and loud, because Aunty says, "My goodness, George, I never heard you so wrought up! I'd almost think you believed that story, child!"

I *was* wound up, though, and I says, "But, Aunty, ain't you never just *felt* like they was some sort of a somethin like a Fool Killer? Ain't you never done things you known was just plumb foolish and kept on doing em even when you seen it, and then you felt like you was going to have to pay the price, and something awful was coming after you?"

She says, "I know that kind of feeling you mean, George, but

145

nothing ever come. I believe it's a person's conscience makes them feel that way."

"But how can you tell? How do you know? You never seen God, but you believe in Him! How do you know they ain't a Fool Killer, just the same way?"

Uncle says, "That's enough, George. Don't talk wild."

Then Milo spoken. He says, "I believe in many things I can't see."

Aunty says, "I reckon most folks does, Mr. Bogardus, but they got to use the sense God give them to decide which them things is to be," and she sounded kind of cross.

Milo says, "I seen many strange things in my life, and many strange things I known without seeing. I ain't prepared to swear that the things I seen was truly there, nor that the things I never seen wasn't."

It was darkening in the kitchen, though 'twas still light enough outside; Milo's eyes was shining back in their caves when they moved; Uncle looked all shadowed out against the door, but Aunty's face took the light so's I could see it plain. Ulysses was laying on his old blanket over by the stove; he set up and begun to scratch his ear, making a thump-thump-thump on the floor. Aunty opened her mouth, shut it, then she made a kind of lady-come-to-see smile like she didn't mean it much.

"Well," she says, "they's certainly many wonders in the world can't nobody explain, and we could discuss them till the cows come home. I just don't want this youngun going off to bed dreaming about eight-foot giants with choppers under their arms. Why, George," she says, and turns to me, "it puts me in mind of the time when I was little and had a spell when I'd yell for Mama ever night because I was sure they was a wolf under my bed. And ever night she'd come upstairs with the candle, just as patient, and get down on her hands and knees to look— and make me get down, too. Wasn't never any wolf there, so I got kind of tired of the idea after a while."

Milo says, "But they could of been. They was wolves in this part the country at one time."

Aunty got up from the table, and Uncle got up, too. "That's right," she says. "My own grandfather shot one and I seen the hide. But they was all gone by my time."

Uncle says to Milo, "You'll have to excuse me, sir, tomorrow I'm picking up a big order over to town, and I got to make room in the store."

Aunty says, "Would you like to take Mr. Bogardus in the parlor, George, while I clean up here?"

I says, "Well—maybe we could walk down and I could show him Bustards' bull, while they's still light."

"If he'd like to," Aunty says, and Milo says, "Fine."

Only I felt like if I stayed there a minute longer I was going to think of something I'd forgot, so I says, "That was awful good chicken, Aunty," but that wasn't it, and I never did think what 'twas; she reached out and rubbed the top of my head where I got the cowlick and says, "Go long."

Milo says, "Thank you, mam," and we went out the door.

32

Evenings was long, now, but we'd et kind of late so the sun was most down. I could hear some of the fellers yelling around towards the other end of town still, though. We cut out back through the fields towards Bustards' pasture. That bull wasn't anything to see—he'd never chased after nobody, not even the time Bessy Silliman climbed over the fence and waved a red shawl on a dare. But I couldn't picture setting in the parlor with Milo waiting for Aunty to finish the dishes. It was kind of gloomy in there, and, in spite of Aunty airing it once a week, it smelled shut up always. Outside, Milo could at least smoke a pipe.

I went ahead, and he come a step or two after me, neither of us saying nothing. *Ain't Aunty and Uncle nice folks?* I started to say, but then I didn't. *Oh, Milo,* I wished I could say to him, *if you only known them the way I do, and if only they known you the same!* The way it was living with them, just busy and peaceful, and not much to tell when you come to try; or all them good times I had with him, working for someone, or playing together, or laying rolled up in our blankets at night, talking, by the fire—yet you couldn't explain how either one was to t'other. Not so's they could understand. *Milo,* I wanted to beg him, *couldn't you stay?* But I known he wouldn't. And if I was to go with him—there'd be my room, and the shipwreck picture with nobody waking up to look at it—or else some other boy . . .

We come to Bustards' pasture, and I says, "There he is." Like I said, wasn't nothing to see, just a old bull cropping the grass and switching off flies. Milo didn't say nothing—wasn't nothing *to* say—we both put our arms on the top rail and he lit his pipe; the two of us stood there staring at the bull like he was a lion in a menagerie. Finally Milo put one foot up on the fence and says in a real quiet voice:

"Well, did you tell them?"

Tell them what? I almost says, but I stopped myself. "No, Milo, no, I ain't had the chance!"

"What do you mean you ain't had the chance?" he says, still in that low voice, like they was somebody sleeping he didn't want to wake. "I waited moren a hour before I followed you."

"I know," I says, "that's right, but don't you see, they'd never even heard of you! They hadn't never asked me nothing, and I hadn't never told them before. So I had to explain about all that—how you and me met up and traveled together, and who you was, and——"

"And what?" he says, real sharp.

"I never told them nothing secret, Milo, I swear! I mentioned how you was in the hospital and forgot everthing from before your wound, on account of I didn't think you'd mind that, but I never told nothing about you having to watch out for enemies! I didn't say nothing wrong, did I, Milo? That part was the only real secret part, far's I known."

He didn't say nothing, just stood pulling on his pipe. Then he says:

"When you going to?"

"Going to what?" says I.

"Tell em."

"I wouldn't never tell em about your enemies! You used to trust me, Milo. What's the matter? What did I do?"

"I don't mean that," he says. "I mean, when you going to tell em you're going with me?"

Then I taken hold of the top rail and tried to shake it. "Milo!" I says. "Oh, Milo, they's things you don't know makes it terrible hard!"

"What things?" says he.

"Like things they done for me and—oh, things is secrets that Aunty told me so I couldn't tell you, Milo, any moren I'd tell her yourn!"

"Say it out, George," he says in that same little low voice. "You ain't coming with me."

"Milo!" I says, only not loud, because his talking so soft

148

made me most whisper, too, "Milo, listen a minute! Milo, don't be mad with me, I can't stand it! Just listen a minute, please! When you gone off after the meeting, I first thought you was dead, or anyways hurt bad, so I searched and searched for you, hoping I could find you and help you in case you was wounded, or anyways find your body if you was dead . . . Milo, don't you remember nothing of what you done then, or how all that blood could of got on the blanket? You must of been hurt some way, or something!"

I had grabbed a piece of his sleeve, but he pulled it out of my hand. "No!" he says. "I don't remember nothing!"

"Well," I says, "anyways, when you wasn't nowheres to be found, and I'd searched so long, I got to wondering—I thought —I mean, I begun to see how a man like you could of got pretty sick of a boy my size tagging along after him all the while."

I waited a minute, but he didn't say nothing.

"Like I'd get tired and want to stop sometimes when you could of gone on further, or lots of times I'll bet you I'd ask you questions when you didn't feel like talking."

Still he never answered me.

"Milo," I says, "when I got to thinking about it, I seen then how I was considerable of a nuisance to you! You was so good to me always it never come to me till after you was gone, but then I could see how it must of been."

"What about Galts?" he says, staring out at the bull, and talking in that little cold-sounding voice. "Ain't you a nuisance to them too?"

"Why," I says, "that's just the thing! They *need* a boy round the place here! I help in the store mornings, and while Uncle takes his nap after dinner; I do chores, and when they got no particular use for me, I'm off with the fellers, out from underfoot!"

Again he didn't answer. I waited a minute, and then I says, "And, Milo—Milo, here's something else I thought of, too——" only the fact was I just thought of it that minute, yet I couldn't see why it had never struck me before "——Supposen you was to want to get married one of these days. You wouldn't want a boy about all the time then, nor your wife neither. You'd be busy raising your own family. 'Tain't like I'd be your real brother so you'd *have* to take me in!"

"What about Galts?" he says. "Supposen they have some children. Where are you then?"

I says, "They ain't going to."

"How do you know?" says he. "They ain't old."

"I can't tell you how, but I know."

Then he taken his arms off the fence and turned round on me with a face so mad-looking I stepped back. They wasn't nothing but black shadows where the eyes should of been, on account of darkness coming down. "Stay with them!" he says, in a whisper like a snake hissing. "Stay, then!"

I felt the tears come in my eyes and run over, and I says, "Don't, Milo, oh, don't!"

"Merchants and money-changers, that's what they are!" he says. "They taken you and changed you, too!"

"What'd you go off and leave me for, then?" I cries. "What'd you expect me to do? You never even give me a warning! You never even said goodbye!"

"You changed!" he says. "You changed! You got the mark of houses and cities and men on you!"

"Oh, don't, Milo!" I says. "I can't help it, if it's so. Just tell me what I ought to do!"

But he turned around and begun running off in the direction of the woods. I run a few steps after him, but I known I could never of catched him, so I fallen right down in the grass there, and howled.

33

'Twas dusk dark by the time I got back, with the frogs going over by the duck pond, and the katydids at it hammer and tongs: *Katy did! She didn't! Didn't! Katy did!* Aunty had a lamp on the kitchen table and was setting by it with her work. The dishes was all put away.

"Why, where's Mr. Bogardus, George?" she says when I come in, the way I expected her to do.

"He went back to his camp," I says, like I'd planned. "He told me to say goodnight and thank you for him. He'd come a long piece today so's he was tired."

"That's a shame when I had the spare room all ready for him! Didn't you tell him he could stay here?"

"He's got so used to camping out he don't care for sleeping in a house no more."

"Well," she says, "I can see how that might be. Why don't you get out the book and read me *The Charge of the Light Brigade* while I finish up hemming this towel?"

"I—I'm tired, too, Aunty. I think I'll go on up to bed now."

I started to go past her, but she reached out, taken my hand, and held me there.

"George," she says, "George, only promise me one thing. If you're going, don't do it without telling me goodbye. I know it's hard, George, but just don't sneak off without telling me."

I felt so tired I could of fell down. I pulled my hand away and backed off from the light. "That's a easy promise, Aunty," I says, "because I ain't going nowheres. Nowheres at all."

"George," she says, starting to get up, but I says, "Good-night, Aunty," and run upstairs.

When I got in bed, I lain on my back looking out on the leaves of the maple tree which got lighter as the moon rose; I listened to the frogs and the katydids and the crickets. I heard Aunty come upstairs and go in her room shortly; after a little she come out again and crossed the hall; my door opened real quiet, but I shut my eyes and pretended I was asleep, and it closed once more. Then I must of dropped off in a doze; I woken with a jump to more footsteps coming creaking up the stairs. I known it was Uncle, walking easy so's not to wake up Aunty and me; at the same time I thought: *That's the Fool Killer out there, eight foot tall with his chopper in his hand, licking his lips and his mouth watering. Come on!* I says to him, inside my head. *Come on and get me! Looks like however I do is the wrong way anyhow!* Then I heard Uncle open the door acrost the hall, and I guess I fell back into a doze; 'twas Aunty's voice woken me next time, saying, "George! George!" I must of been dreaming she was beside my bed, because when I opened my eyes, I was surprised not to find her there. Then I heard her voice again, little and soft but plain calling, "George, George!"

I thrown back the covers, jumped out of bed, opened my door, and went out in the hall. The door to their room had been left open; the moon was shining in their window brighten a lamp. I could see the patchwork quilt folded over the footboard of their bed with all its patches which looked so gay in daylight washed out to no colors you could name; when I stood in the door, I seen how the footboard thrown a black shadow like a cover pulled up to Aunty's waist on the bed; above it, she rose up all white in the moonlight, in her nightgown, with her hair down in a braid, propped up on her elbows against the bolster. And she was so still she didn't look real; she didn't even turn her head when she heard me there; she just says, "Don't say nothing, George. Don't say a word. Go downstairs as quiet as you know how and get Uncle." Her voice was so little and soft I couldn't hardly hear it, yet the words come to me clear and plain, and the way she spoken didn't leave no room for doubt that I must do just what she said, as fast as I could go, without asking why.

Then I turned to go, but just in the second I was moving away, I seen the moon catch on something flat and shiny in the shadow by the window—it made me turn back to look again, which was when I made out a shape—a great tall figure standing still in the shadows, with the moon catching on the flat of a ax-head it was holding in its hands.

Then I run for the head of the stairs; going down them I felt like a swaller diving through the air; I raced down the hall to the store and found Uncle setting all peaceful beside the lamp, with his specs on, figgering at his books.

I run at him and grabbed his arm. "Come!" I says, but no voice come out my throat, so I jerked at him and made him up-set the ink bottle on the page.

"What?" he says, and begun to get up slow.

I says, "Come! Come quiet! Bring the gun!"

Then I went flying back in the hall; I pulled over a chair and was climbing on it to reach down the shotgun was kept loaded at the top of the gun rack, but he was there reaching it down be-fore I got to it; I run up the stairs with him right behind me, most as quiet as my bare feet in his carpet slippers. At the top, I just pointed to their room, and he shoved me behind him to step in the door.

Wasn't no sound but different breathing, and noises outside in the night. I heard Aunty say in that little low voice, "Don't move, Samuel. Don't do nothing unless you must."

I leaned forward to see round him, and there she was, just like I'd left her. I could see the sleeve of her nightgown quiver-ing like she was in a awkward position and her arm had got tired. Beyond her, in the shadow by the window, was the sharp glint in the moonlight again, and when my eyes got used to the dark, the great tall figure standing, holding the ax. Then I seen it move; it taken a step forwards; Uncle says, "Stay where you

152

are!" so loud I jumped, and put the gun up to his shoulder; I ducked under his arm and into the room.

"Milo!" I cries, running towards him, and they was a loud noise of the ax falling to the floor. For a minute he stood with his hands out the way they had been holding it, like a blind man; then, quick's a cat, just as I touched him, he whirled round and skinned out the open window, big as he was, and jumped across to the eaves of the ell.

"Milo!" I yells, and stuck my head out the window. "Come back!" But he was clambering up the shingles, slipping and sliding, till he come to the peak of the roof. There he stood up like on a mountaintop, one foot on each side.

I had my leg over the windowsill to go after him, but Uncle grabbed me round the waist from behind and held me fast.

"Milo!" I called out again, kicking and struggling, "Milo, come back!" but he never turned. He stood up from the roof, looking tallern any man, with the full moon little and high over his head, shining its light down on him so he was all black and white, like a statue. Then I seen him take a step, and another, balancing along the roof until he come to the end; there he put out his arms like a bird spreading its wings to fly, he made a loud, kind of wailing cry, and jumped, straight out into the air.

34

I can't tell you just how soon after that it was that I was took with the fever and was sick for the rest of the summer, because I was out of my head a lot of the time which made me forget the way things had happened, or mix them up, sometimes. I was so bad nobody could see me then but Aunty and the doctor; they shaved off all my hair, but it grown in again. The first I can remember clear was when the fever was just gone and Aunty used to bring her work in my room afternoons and set rocking there. We didn't talk, though, because I felt so tired all the time I didn't even want to say yes or no.

Except for one day, when I wasn't expecting to say nothing

153

at all, I heared myself asking, "Did he die?" just like that, and Aunty says:

"Yes, George."

"I'm glad!" I says. "He weren't nothing but a murderer! He was fixing to kill you!" and the tears begun rolling down my face, like I could never keep them from doing, around that time.

Aunty says, "Hush, George!" and got up to give me some medicine, and set on the bed holding my hand until I went off to sleep.

Then, for a long time, it looked like I lain in bed day after day, not wanting to eat, or talk, or move, or do nothing; Aunty was always carrying me eggnogs till I hated the sight of the things; one day she brought Ulysses upstairs; he jumped on my bed and begun licking my face, but it just seemed like more than I could stand; the tears begun again, and I says, "Take him away!"

Evenings, Uncle would come to set with me, and I would be glad for how he never said nothing much, though sometimes he would read out loud.

But finally, one time, when he'd been setting there quiet for a spell, he says, "George," and I says:

"Yes, sir."

He cleared his throat and says, "You been through a bad time."

I says, "I reckon I'm getting better, though. Aunty says maybe I can set up in the chair next week."

He says, "That ain't what I mean."

I known he meant Milo, then, and I kept mum, for I didn't want to talk of that, no, nor think of it, nor hear of it, ever any more.

It was like he heard me thinking, for he says, "You got to talk of it, George."

I turned my face away so's he couldn't see it, and I says, "What's there to say?"

"You liked that feller, didn't you?"

I couldn't answer, because them blamed tears had begun again. Finally I got hold on myself enough to say, "You don't need to tell me he weren't no good! I seen him after Aunty with the ax! He'da kilt her, too, if you hadn't gotten there!"

"But that don't change him being good to you before."

Then I flopped over, pulled the pillow over my head, and reglar howled; I heard Uncle creaking acrost the floor and felt the mattress sink down beside me.

"Go way!" I hollers. "Leave me alone!" But maybe he couldn't hear me from where I was under the pillow. Finally he pulled it off me, taken my shoulder and turned me over; pulled out his handkerchief and given it to me. When I handed it back after I blown, I seen his face was working like a first-grader spelling out a hard word.

"Things held inside can poison a person," he says. "I know."

I didn't answer nor look at him, and he didn't say nothing more neither for a time.

Then all of a sudden I busts out, "I believe 'twas him kilt the preacher at the camp meeting! I been laying here thinking how I half known it all the time, only I kept making up them crazy tales about the Fool Killer, or believed in them enemies of his nobody never seen, just to diddle myself!"

Uncle says, "I thought of that, too, but I guess no one'll ever know for sure. But even if 'twas so, George, it don't look to me like he done it in cold blood. When he taken them spells like you told of, sounded to me like he was clean out of his mind. You can't blame him for what he done then, no moren you'd blame Ulysses for biting if he taken the hydrophobia."

Then I begun to blubber again, not even hiding my face. "He *was* good to me!" I says. "He—he teached me to make willow whistles! He'd always notice if I was tired and stop to make camp without I even said a word! At night we'd lay by the fire talking, and he used to say we was like brothers! I felt like it, too, only 'twas me kilt him, yelling at him that way, just like Cain kilt Abel!"

"Now wait a minute!" Uncle says, taking a grip on my wrist and holding it hard. "Just stop right there! That don't make no sense whatever. You was trying to prevent him, and you failed, but that don't make you responsible!"

"Ain't that what Cain said, too?" I bellers. "Am I my brother's keeper?"

"Well," says Uncle, and let go my wrist. He put his hands on his knees, and for a minute I was afraid he was going off and leave me there. He didn't say nothing more, and I didn't look at him, just lain there sniveling and hiccupping, with the tears running down. Then he spoken again, and his voice sounded altogether different, more like I've heared it when some man come to ask his advice in the store, just kind of thoughtful and calm.

"Well, George," says he, "looks like here's a case where they ain't nothing for it but to pull yourself up by your own bootstraps and start in to be a man."

I says, blubbering, "I—I don't know how!"

He says, "I don't reckon nobody could give you a exact recipe, but I'll tell you the best I know. Seems to me like you got to look at the facts and look at em straight, but not go play-acting off in this direction and that, making out things is worse than they are when they're bad enough to begin with. You seen some dreadful things happen. I'm pretty nigh fifty years old and never run into nothing like them before. Ain't no wonder if you don't know what to make of em, for I ain't sure I could tell you. Only this much I do know: ain't no use laying here turning yourself inside out over your fault, his fault, t'other one's fault; and it ain't no use brooding over dreadfulness, neither. You got to think of them good times when he was a friend to you, and try your level best to put the awful ones out of your mind. Enjoy the good and stand up to the bad—that's the best I can tell you how to be a man."

"I can't!" I says. "How can I forget him standing there in the dark with a ax and Aunty——"

"Just stop it!" he says. "Maybe you can't forget it right away. But you can try, stead of dwelling on it like you was biting on a sore tooth all day. Now I'm going to call your aunty to put you to bed." And he got up and left.

Then I felt so mad I quit bawling, and I downright hated Uncle for talking that way. Did he think I could shut off parts of my mind like they had lids to em? Did he think a person could just put a idea out of his head like you'd put a dog outdoors? *Have* you *forgot it?* I wish I'd asked him. I'd forget them things when I was wounded in the head and had my memory washed away like Milo—not before!

Yet the funny thing was, that night, after Aunty come and fixed me up for bed and set by me until I went to sleep, I dreamed of Milo, and for the first time since I got sick, 'tweren't a awful dream. I dreamed we was swimming together at the swimming hole, swinging on the grapevine swing, doing tricks on the bank, and laying laughing afterwards the way we used to do; then, at the end, we put on our clothes, and he says, "Well, so long!" and went off waving at me, while I turned home with Ulysses. Next morning when I woke up from it, I felt so hungry I et three eggs, and after that was when I really started in to feeling better every day.

I don't mean I forgot them terrible times and never thought of them no more, only, from then on, they was easier to talk of, even when they'd make me cry. Once I asked Aunty how God could of let such things happen, and she says, "He's got a plan we fit in biggern anything we can see," and though that didn't satisfy me much, I could see how they probly wasn't nothing else even a minister or Milo hisself could of said.

Then, in a week or so, I was setting up in the rocker and they let Bill Bustard and St. Elmo in to see me, first only one at a time, and each one walking on his tippy toes like I was a funeral; before the time school begun, I was back working in the store and doing my chores like always; after I was up and around, Aunty had to make me all new clothes because I'd outgrowed the old before they was even wore out.

Then it was fall; school begun, us fellers'd rake up leaves in piles and jump in em so's we'd have to rake them all over again to make bonfires; on Halloween we went round and tipped over Parkmans' privy; in school we come to parsing and percents; one day I dipped Alice Ferris' pigtail in the ink for a paintbrush, but Teacher caught me at it and kept me in for a week. Whiskey Pete built him a new still in the haunted house which Bill and me found but never told; Bessy Silliman married a feller from over to Deepwell, and all us boys went along in the wagon on the shivaree; Uncle walked in on me one day when I was trying out his razor and scared me so I cut myself, but he only laughed and says don't nick his blade on that pirate's beard I got there.

Excepting it ain't like that all the time no more. Sometimes, these days, I feel like I just got to go up to my room and shut the door and be off to myself to think of things. Then I lay on my bed, and it's like I was some place high up in the sky, looking down on everthing and everbody, a million miles away. I think of Milo, then, both the good things and the bad, only it don't make me feel so awful, the way it used to do; I think of how many strange things has happened to me in my life, and I feel like I'm a old man, compared with them fellers in school has never been nowhere nor seen nothing outside this place and maybe the next town . . .

Then I get a awful restless feeling at how peaceful and kind of uninteresting things has got to be; I jump up off my bed and go out to split stove wood for Aunty, or roust out St. Elmo and Bill, and I oftentimes think that if it wasn't for Uncle and Aunty needing me here, I'd probly hit the road again, come spring.

A CRIME CLUB SELECTION

DARK LADY
By Doris Miles Disney

A CRIME CLUB SELECTION

The 7th Mourner
A MYSTERY BY DOROTHY GARDINER

A CRIME CLUB SELECTION

DEATH & CHICANERY

The Doubleday CRIME CLUB® has always been your guarantee of the very best in hard cover mysteries. Now, for the first time, Popular Library makes a series of outstanding CRIME CLUB titles available in paperback at all newsstands and book stores.

W1144   75c

THE
Conquering
Family

Thomas B. Costain
A great storyteller at his best

Author of THE BLACK ROSE and THE SILVER CHALICE

A MAJOR NATIONWIDE BESTSELLER

"BRILLIANT...SWIFT-MOVING."
—BOOK-OF-THE-MONTH CLUB NEWS

First in the brilliant series including
THE LAST PLANTAGENETS
A Popular Library Bestseller—only 75c